I0539745

MABEL OR THE BITTER ROOT

OH, HERE SHE COMES!
BUT WHO IS THAT HOLDING HER HAND? (PAGE 17.)

MABEL

OR

THE BITTER ROOT

A TALE OF THE TIMES OF JAMES THE FIRST

BY

LUCY ELLEN GUERNSEY

MINNEAPOLIS

2010

Published by Curiosmith.
P. O. Box 390293, Minneapolis, Minnesota, 55439.
Internet: curiosmith.com.
E-mail: shopkeeper@curiosmith.com.

Previously published in 1869 by The American Sunday-School Union.

Supplementary content and cover design:
Copyright © 2010 Charles J. Doe.

ISBN 9781935626039

CONTENTS

I.   THE STRANGER.............................. 9

II.   THE SCHOOL FEAST. 20

III. THE LACE-MAKING. 38

IV.   THE SECRET GRIEF......................... 53

V.   THE PERSECUTION.......................... 66

VI.   THE HOUSEWIFE............................ 80

VII. THE ROOT BEARS FRUIT.................... 94

VIII. ON THE CLIFF............................. 115

PREFACE

THE present story is intended to illustrate one phase of English history, and that a very terrible one,—I mean the persecutions for witchcraft, in the time of James the First. It is true that witches were hung and burned both before and after the days of the Scottish Solomon; but James was the only monarch who took the superstition, as it were, under his personal patronage; and during his reign nobody was safe from an accusation of sorcery. Was a woman remarkably old and withered, or unusually young and pretty for her age,—was she too ignorant to say the Lord's Prayer correctly, or did she know more than her neighbors,—was she lucky or subject to be considered a witch, and persecuted accordingly. The art of *witch-finding* was a regular trade, and the wretches who practiced it made it a lucrative profession.

It may readily be seen what a weapon was thus put into the hands of ignorance and malice. It was easy for a man who hated his neighbor for any cause to bring up against him an accusation of sorcery, and as his innocence was only proved by his sinking in the water wherein he was plunged, he was sure to lose his life at any rate.

There is no danger now of any one's being persecuted for witchcraft; but it is well now and then to cast back a look at the condition of society in past centuries, if it be only to enable us to appreciate our own present comforts and security, which we are prone to consider altogether a matter of course.

L. E. G.

CHAPTER I

THE STRANGER

ON a beautiful June morning, in the year 1625, a group of school-girls of all ages, from six up to fifteen, were collected around the door of the school-house at Stantoun-Corbet, waiting for the mistress. A very pretty picture they made, in their green stuff dresses, white bibs, and red hoods and tippets. You must not imagine that they looked at all like the crowd you may see about the door of a public-school nowadays, or that the school-house resembled one of those huge brick erections which are to be found in every ward of our cities, or the little square school-house in a country district. Lady Rosamond's school—as the institution was called—had been erected in the reign of Elizabeth, nearly seventy years before. It was built of dark red sandstone, with thick walls, and a high pitched roof, with a little belfry at one end, and a deep stone porch. The windows were filled with small diamond-shaped panes of glass, set in lead frames, while in the middle of each one a larger compartment was painted, with the crest of the Stantoun family, surrounded by the pious motto of the house, "God is our hope!" One end of the house was covered with luxuriant ivy, climbing to the very roof, while at the other grew a beautiful elm tree. The girls were always dressed in uniform,—green frocks, red hoods, very simply made, and white bibs, which it was the pride of Lady Rosamond's school-girls to wear for a whole week without soiling.

The school had been built in the second year of the reign of Queen Elizabeth, by the young heiress Lady

Rosamond Stantoun, as a thank-offering for the deliver-
ance of herself and her friends from great danger, and
was by her endowed for the education—in reading and
writing, in sewing and other handiworks, as well as in the
Old and New Testament history and the doctrines of the
Church of England—of forty young girls, from the age of
five to fifteen, the said girls being taken from the village
of Stantoun-Corbet, and the two neighboring hamlets of
Freshwater Cove and Millheads. The mistress was to be
appointed by the Countess of Stantoun, or, failing her, by
the lady of Corby-End. She had usually been some depen-
dant of the family at the court, sometimes a waiting gentlewoman or housekeeper, sometimes a distant relative.
The present incumbent was rather a superior person,
the orphan daughter of a clergyman in Exeter. Elizabeth
Ellenwood was a lady by birth and education, and some
people wondered that she could be contented to spend her
days the mistress of a village school in such a corner of
the world as Stantoun-Corbet, when she had the choice of
going to London in the train of the Bishop's lady of Exeter,
and perhaps of making a grand match. But Elizabeth
Ellenwood had no desire to make a grand match, or to see
London. Her heart had gone down in the deep sea, with
one who had sailed with Sir Walter Raleigh on his last
desperate adventure. She had no fancy for gayeties and
no desire to be a dependent upon the Bishop's lady. So she
thankfully accepted the offer made by her far-away cousin, Lady Stantoun, and with her chief treasures—some
remains of her father's library and her mother's antique
cabinets and oaken furniture—she settled herself in the
stone cottage attached to the school, and prepared to give
her whole mind to teaching the little ones committed to
her charge.

Mrs. Ellenwood presented a great contrast to the
old dame who had preceded her. Dame Huson used to
doze away her time in the school-room on school-days as
she dozed by her fireside, and in her seat in church on

Sundays and holidays; and, provided they did not make
noise enough to wake her up, the girls might carry on
what games they pleased. Mistress Ellenwood's eyes and
ears seemed to be everywhere at once, and no idler or
mischief-maker could be sure to remain unseen for two
minutes at a time. Dame Huson looked upon lessons as a
troublesome interruption, to be got through as quickly as
possible, while to Mistress Ellenwood they were clearly
the great business of life. She neither slighted them herself nor allowed any one else to do so; and while she had
endless patience with real dullness or incapacity, she was
very decided with all idlers and blunderers. In the course
of three months she had made an entire revolution in the
school. The Bible lessons were no longer stammered or
gabbled over, with no sense of the meaning of the sacred
word, and no object save to get through the task as soon
as possible. The chapter must be studied beforehand, and
read slowly and with reverence, and Mistress Ellenwood
always questioned the girls about what they had read.
The sewing, the knitting, the spinning, must be done
neatly and exactly, or all was to be picked out and done
again.

It may be guessed that this revolution was not effect-
ed without some grumbling; but there was no attempt at
open rebellion. Mistress Ellenwood's manner, though always kind and gentle, overawed her subjects a good deal,
and caused the discontent to confine itself to private mur-
murings at the new-fangled ways, and now and then a
shower of tears over a hard lesson or a bit of unpicking. It
was observed, that the brightest girls of the school were
soon all enlisted on the side of the new mistress, and no
one more decidedly than Mabel Winne. Mabel was fifteen
years old, and had for a long time been the head girl of the
school. She was the only daughter of a well-to-do farmer
and was likely to be a bit of an heiress, and she had also
expectations from an uncle and aunt, a childless old cou-
ple, and reported rich. Master Jasper Winne and his wife

were fond of Mabel, and made much of her; and it was generally believed that at their death the bit of land and the comfortable cottage, as well as the old man's savings, would fall to Mabel. All this helped to make the girl of importance in the little community. But there were other and better reasons for Mabel's popularity. Though somewhat imperious and given to wanting her own way upon all occasions, she was good-natured and generous, ever ready to help a friend in distress, or to share her cake or apple. If a girl found a hard word in her lesson, or a knot in her thread, or had made a misstitch in her sampler, she carried her book or her work to Mabel Winne; and Mabel, while she scolded at her stupidity, never failed to do her best to help her out. Mabel sometimes complained of the trouble the girls gave her; but she would not have been at all pleased to find herself relieved of this trouble.

Mabel was very decided in all her likings and dislikings, and she had taken to the new mistress at once. Mistress Ellenwood was a very handsome woman, to begin with, and Mabel was fond of every thing beautiful. Then she was always somewhat sad and reserved, associating little with the neighbors, and spending her time over a book, or in walk—up and down her little garden, while all the villagers were assembled on the green to criticize the dancers, or watch the wrestling, or the single-stick players. Then Mistress Ellenwood knew more than any person Mabel had ever met of that great world outside of Devonshire, outside even of England, about which curiosity was so powerfully excited among all classes. She owned some books of travels, and had read many more, and she had actually received letters from Spain, Italy, and even from Jerusalem,—a fact which powerfully impressed the mind of the school-girl whose longest journey had been a ride to Biddeford or Langham on a pillion behind her father or uncle.

Mabel had always heretofore looked upon the every-day Bible lesson as a tiresome but necessary duty, to be got rid of as quickly as possible, while at the same time she had an uneasy feeling that the Bible was the word of God, after all, and ought to be treated with respect. But Mistress Ellenwood made a very different matter of it. She told the children the meaning of all the hard words. She seemed, by her manner of speaking, to make the personages of the sacred story live and move familiarly before them, and she brought to illustrate the lessons many facts which she had meet with in her reading. Moreover, she aroused in their minds the conviction that the Bible was the rule of life, the word and witness of God himself, and that it contained messages to them in particular. A new spirit began by degrees to grow up in Lady Rosamond's school,—a sense of duty and right which worked wonders in bringing about the changes which Elizabeth Ellenwood ardently desired to see. There was less of quarrelling among the girls, less lying and petty gossiping, and more readiness in helping one another. To some among them, the prayers with which the school was always opened began to seem something less like a tiresome task and more like an address to a real living person capable of understanding and supplying their wants,—seeing and pardoning or else punishing their sins.

To Mabel especially the change was very great. She had a bright and active mind, and a naturally warm admiration for every thing beautiful, which had hitherto found little matter upon which to be exercised. True, nothing could be more picturesque than the lanes and woods, the cliffs and shore, in the neighborhood of Stantoun-Corbet. The great wild moor lifted itself almost like a mountain-range on the horizon on one side, and the waters of the Atlantic Ocean rose up like a wall on the other, so high did the little village stand above the shore. But Mabel had lived in the midst of these things all her life, and no one had taught her to admire them. People do not usually have, as somebody says, "a natural taste for the beauties of nature," and such a taste was far from common at that day and for long afterwards, even among cultivated people. When Mr. Evelyn traveled through the passes of the Alps, some twenty years after the date of my tale, he could find nothing to admire in that scenery which now attracts thousands of people every year. It was not to be expected that the little Devon school-girl should be wiser than her betters; and she thought of the sea only as a place to catch fish, and a road to the Indies, the cliffs as places where the boys were always getting into scrapes going after birds' nests. The woods were nice to go nut-ting in, when the steward was kind enough to permit such an indulgence, and the banks of the lane furnished prim-roses and violets, periwinkle and rose campions, for nose-gays, and a variety of medicinal herbs for her mother's simple pharmacy. To the moor, indeed, she looked with awe; but it was because her fancy peopled it with all sorts of strange and supernatural beings, besides its half wild and, as many believed, half brutish human inhabitants, who had power to bewitch cattle, to shoot sheep with elf-arms and thunder-bolts, and to cause the death, by magic or slow poison, of any one who offended them.

But Mabel's mind opened rapidly under the influ-ence brought to bear upon it by Elizabeth Ellenwood. She learned to associate the evening star with that guiding star which led the wise men to the stable at Bethlehem. She learned to see beauty in sunsets and sunrises, such as she had never thought of before; to consider the great cliffs and yellow sands as the bounds set for the waters, "that they turn not again to cover the earth," and by de-grees to enter into the spirit of that wonderful poem of nature, the one hundred and fourth psalm. Nor was that all. Mabel learned to know something of her heavenly Father's love and goodness, as shown in the gift of his dear Son to die for sinners; she began to have some appre-ciation of his character and to desire to serve and please him. She had not gone so far as to feel her own personal need of this Savior. Indeed, Mabel fancied herself a very good girl, especially now that she had begun to say her prayers and to read her Bible understandingly. But she felt the delight natural to an active mind and imagination, of having a new and wide field opened for their exercise, and she loved with a kind of passionate adoration the one who had conferred upon her this benefit.

This adoration on Mabel's part was not without its inconveniences. Mabel would fain have kept the mistress all to herself, and was disposed to be jealous and offended when Elizabeth showed favor to any one else; when she suffered the little ones to cluster around her while she walked from the school-house to her own cottage; when she stopped to hear Polly Bell tell of the twin calves born to her mother's favorite cow, or Jane Lee give an account of the strange fish her father had brought ashore in his boat "down to fresh water." Elizabeth was fond of Mabel, and took great pleasure in observing and aiding the opening of her mind and heart; but she loved the other girls as well, and especially delighted in the prattle of the little ones. Moreover, Elizabeth sometimes felt the need of solitude after and before the labors of the day, and she was obliged to make a rule that none of the children must come to her house uninvited. Though this rule was general in its operation, Mabel felt it peculiarly hard upon herself, and was disposed to resent it as a personal injury. However, there was no help for it, and she was obliged to submit.

On the morning on which our story opened, Mabel was not among the girls who were clustering (like bees about a hive) around the door and porch of the school-house and under the elm tree. It was the king's birthday, and a holiday, upon which occasions the children went to church with their mistress, and were examined for an hour upon the Catechism and the Bible, by the rector, or the master of the boy's school, after which the day was their own. This, however, was a special occasion, for my lady had come home from London, and had invited all the girls and boys, with their master and mistress, to come up to a feast of cakes, curds-and-cream, and other good things, upon the lawn at Stantoun-Corbet. Such a thing had not happened before for a long time, for the last Lady Stantoun had lived mostly in London, and had never shown any great interest in the school. It was understood, however, that the present lady was a very different sort of person, and that the new Lord Stantoun intended to live almost entirely upon his estate,—a piece of news which gave great satisfaction to everyone in the parish, except the steward, who foresaw that his power would be considerably abridged.

It was drawing towards nine o'clock. The church clock had struck the three-quarters, and many were the impatient and wondering glances cast towards the gate of the stone cottage.

"What does keep the mistress so long?" said Jane Lee. "We shall be late for church as sure as there's fish in the sea; and then what will parson say?"

"We have never been late once since Mistress Ellenwood came!" remarked another. "We never have to go and wake her, as we used to do with Dame Huson. Do you remember, Janey, how we went after her once, and found her asleep on the style?"

"No danger of that with mistress nowadays!" said Cicely Hood, who lived next door to the stone cottage. "I often hear her singing in her garden before I am up, and such beautiful grand tunes! 'Tis like the angels!" added Cicely, with enthusiasm.

"Much you know about angels!"

"I know that they sing, and that they are good and beautiful, for it says so in the Bible? So there, Polly Briggs!" retorted Cicely, good-humoredly holding her own. "And I am certain that mistress is good and beautiful both!"

"Ay, that she is! That's you, Cicely!" assented several girls, while only one added, "only so desperately tedious and particular."

"She is not a bit tedious and particular, if you will only mind what you are about!" said the champion Cicely. "You only say so because she made you unpick your dog's tail in your sampler, and you had worked it clear across the canvas. Who ever saw a dog with his tail four times as long as his body?"

"Who ever saw a dog one bit like the dogs we work in our samplers, any way!" retorted Anne, not without some show of reason. "I am sure I never did."

"You need not make them more unlike, then! Besides, they are not meant to be. If they were exactly like real dogs, where would be the use in working them? We can see real dogs any day, without taking all that trouble," said Cicely, unconsciously enunciating one of the rules of a great school of artists.

But all this time what became of mistress?

"Oh, here she comes at last, and Mabel with her. How fond Mabel is of mistress, to be sure! But who is that holding her other hand? I never saw her before. I am sure she does not live about here."

The girls had ample time to speculate upon the appearance of the stranger, who walked slowly across the green holding the hand of the mistress, who was talking to Master Jasper Winne. She was small and delicate-looking, dressed in deep mourning of rather fine quality, and the deep black hood she wore concealed her face. As she came nearer, the girls saw that she was somewhat lame. Mabel walked on the other side of the mistress, and the girls fancied that she did not look very well pleased.

"I wonder who she is!" said Cicely.

"Some relation of the mistress, come to live with her, perhaps!"

"We shall soon know; so there is no use in guessing," observed Jane.

"I have brought you a new playmate, girls," said the mistress, as she came up to the group of scholars, who were dropping their courtesies to herself and Master

Jasper. "This is Isabel Gray who has come to live with Master Winne and his wife, and she will be your school-mate. Let me see how kind you can be to the stranger! Now, get yourself in order, and we will set out for church, for we have no time to lose. Mabel, you may walk with Cicely today and as Isabel is a stranger, I will take her with me!"

Mabel did not refuse to obey, but she looked far from being pleased. It was her privilege, as head girl, to walk with the mistress in all the little processions of the school. It had not been a coveted or desirable office under Dame Huson, who crawled like a snail, frequently stumbled, and was always late; but with this mistress it was very different, and Mabel felt a little like a dethroned princess. To do her justice, she tried to overcome the feeling; but she did not entirely succeed, and she was conscious in her heart of being a little jealous of the stranger.

There were more reasons than one for the feeling. Mabel had always been a pet with her uncle Jasper and his wife, and from hearing the matter so often mentioned, she had come to consider herself as his rightful heir. But some little time before, Master Jasper had set out on a long journey, without telling any one but his wife where he was going. He had not even taken his old serving-man Peter, and many were the head-shakings and the doubt-ful hopes expressed by his old cronies under the tree at the Chequers, that the old man would come home all right after making such a venture at his age.

But all expectations of disaster were destined to be dis-appointed. Master Jasper had come home in safety two or three days before, bringing on a pillion behind him a new inmate for the comfortable old Red House,—a little fair-haired girl, who was received with warm affection by old Dame Winne, and by her introduced to some neighbors who dropped in, as "my grand-niece Isabel, come to live with Jasper and me, in our old age,—bless her!" Isabel herself seemed a pretty timid child, shy of strangers to a painful degree, and shrinking close to the side of her aunt when any one so much as looked at her. She had never stirred out of doors till the evening that our story commences, when Master Jasper took her to the school cottage, and presented her to the mistress.

CHAPTER II

THE SCHOOL FEAST

THE Church service being ended, the boys and girls were ranged in order in the pews, to be catechized by the pastor himself. Isabel, as being a stranger, was excused for this time, and sat quietly at the side of the mistress, apparently more interested in gazing at the famous east window of the church—which strangers came even from Exeter and Plymouth to see—than in listening to the catechizing. Only once did she show any particular feeling. It was when the worthy pastor, at the end of the lesson, alluded to the proposed school feast, given by the excellent lady at the court, in honor of the birthday of our excellent monarch, King James the First, whom may God long preserve in health and wealth! The mistress happened to be looking at Isabel as the words were spoken, and was surprised at the change in the child's face. The color mounted to her cheeks, her large gray eyes seemed to flash with indignation, and her lips were compressed, while at the same time her head was slightly shaken, as if to mark her utter dissent from the loyal words of the minister. In a minute her eyelids dropped, her color faded, and the large tears stole out from under her long lashes, while her bosom and whole frame seemed shaken with suppressed sobs. With a desperate struggle, however, she recovered her former composure of manner, though her eyes were no longer fixed upon the painted window, but cast down to the ground.

"What ails the child?" thought the mistress; but her attention was presently diverted by the dismission of the children, and the little bustle attendant upon forming the line—for the drill was as rigid as could be—and getting the girls out of church in an orderly manner.

The girls were to meet at the school-house again at one o'clock, and while the mistress was enjoining upon her flock the necessity of appearing with the cleanest of hands and faces and whitest of caps and bibs, the parson came up, and made his regular formal compliment to the mistress on the excellence of her management and the proficiency of her scholars. No one had rejoiced more over the change of the mistress than Parson Parnell. Elizabeth's father had been his friend in college; so, as he said, he began to like her for her father's sake, and ended in loving her for her own.

"And who is this fair young maid?" he asked, laying his hand upon the head of Isabel.

"This is a new scholar, a grand-niece of Master Jasper," replied the mistress. The pastor nodded gravely.

"Ay, ay! I comprehend. Master Jasper spoke somewhat to me! The blessing of the God of the fatherless be upon thee, my maid!" he added again, laying his hand upon her head. Isabel looked up to him with a grateful smile, which seemed for the moment to light up her face like sunshine.

"How pretty she is!" said Cicely, aside, to Mabel Winne. "It will be nice to have a cousin; won't it?"

"She is not my cousin!" returned Mabel, coldly. "She is no blood relation to me."

"But she is a kind of cousin, after all!" persisted Cicely. "And you will see a good deal of her, being so much at your uncle's as you are. Don't you think you shall like her, Mabel?"

"What a silly question!" said Mabel, sharply. "How can I tell whether I shall like her or not? I have only seen her twice."

"Anyhow, you need not be so cross!" said Cicely.

"Nonsense! I am not cross; but I don't like you to be silly! See, now, there is parson going into the school-room, to see our work, I dare say. I am glad your nice 'kerchief is so nearly done, Cicely!"

The diversion proved effectual, as Mabel intended, and Cicely thought no more about the stranger.

"Mabel, you had better call for your cousin," said the mistress, pausing for a moment at the school-house door. "She is a stranger among us, you know, and we must take care to make her feel at home."

"It is out of my way!" said Mabel. "Cicely lives nearer."

"Oh, I will bring her!" said good-natured Cicely. "I am sure she will come with me. Won't you, Isabel?"

"Thank you, Cicely. I shall be glad for you to show Isabel all the kindness you are able; but it is Mabel's business, as head girl, to introduce the stranger into the way of the school, and it should be her pride to fulfill it, especially to her cousin!"

"She is not my cousin!" murmured Mabel.

"Mabel!" said the mistress, looking at her in surprise and with a reproving expression: "what does this mean? Must I speak twice to you; and do you presume to return me an answer? Recollect yourself, maiden!"

Mabel colored to the roots of her crispy black hair at the reproof, and seemed about to make a still sharper reply; but, controlling herself, she curtsied and stood in silence.

"Please, mistress!" said Isabel, speaking for the first time, "I would rather not go to the feast. Cicely is very good: so is Mabel; but I should like to stay at home."

"And why so, sweet-heart?"

"I am a stranger!" said Isabel, "and—and—I am not dressed like the rest!" she added, with a tremor in her voice, casting a glance at her black frock. "Perhaps my lady would not like to see me among them!"

"Still, Isabel, I think you had better go," said the mistress, kindly. "My lady particularly wishes to see all the children, and I fear she would not be pleased if you stayed away. I am sure, girls, you will all be kind to Isabel, and help her to enjoy herself."

"Yes, mistress! Yes indeed, mistress!" replied most of the girls, heartily; but Mabel said not a word. She seemed engaged in a struggle with herself; and as the mistress turned into the school-room, she spoke abruptly, but with an evident effort at good-nature.

"Come, Cicely, we will take Isabel home between us. Come, Isabel!"

"Are you to live at Master Jasper's for good?" asked Cicely, presently.

"Yes; I suppose so: I have no other place to live," replied Isabel, sadly; and then, as if fearing she had spoken ungraciously, she added, "Uncle Jasper and Aunt Bell are very good to me, and I think this a pretty place. The sea is so beautiful! I never saw it before."

"Why, where can you have lived?" asked Cicely, in a tone of surprise. She had never been out of the sight and sound of the ocean.

"I lived near Malvern, in Worcestershire," replied Isabel. "There is no sea, but there are beautiful hills and streams, and such great trees! And there are fine wells, where people come to drink and bathe in the waters,—even from London sometimes!"

"Didn't you hate to come away?" asked Cicely.

"No!" replied Isabel, with the same curious flash of the eyes and compression of the lips which the mistress had noticed in church. "I was glad to come away, and I never want to go back again—NEVER!" she repeated, with emphasis.

"Why, were not the people good to you?" Cicely began; but Mabel interrupted her.

"Don't ask so many questions, Cicely! What a chatterbox you are?"

"She did not mean any harm!" said Isabel, slipping her hand into that of Cicely, who looked rather abashed. "Only please, girls, don't ask me about Malvern just now. My mother died there," she added, with an apparently painful effort.

"To be sure, poor thing!" said Cicely, sympathetically. "I am sure I should not know what to do if my mother were to die. But here we are, and here is Dame Winne looking out for us. Here is Isabel, dame! we have brought her safe home."

"Ay, ay, dears! So my maid has found friends already! That is right," said the kindly old woman. "Just wait a bit." She hobbled into the house, and soon returned with three or four goodly-sized currant-buns.

"Here, eat a bit; I made them only this morning. Take this to thy little sister, Cicely. Come, Mabel; come in and have thy dinner with us! Uncle will be glad to see his maid, and I have a nice fat hen in the pot."

But Mabel excused herself. Her mother would expect her home, she said; and, promising to call for Isabel at half-past twelve, she hastened away.

"Well, and how did you like your school and your mistress?" asked Dame Winne.

"I like the mistress," answered Isabel, "and the girls seem good-natured; only they stare at me so, and its all so strange!"

"Yes; to be sure, poor maid!" said Dame Winne; "but you will soon feel at home. Run out now to the orchard, and call thy uncle to dinner."

Punctually at half-past twelve Mabel called at the Red House for Isabel.

"Look at them!" said Dame Winne to her husband, as they stood together in the porch.

"Don't they look like the red and white rose out in Parson's garden?"

"Mabel is like the rose, if you please!" answered Jasper. "But Isabel is more, to my mind, like the white birdweed in the hedge. There is no fault to be found with the outside either way. But beauty is only skin deep, maids! Remember that!" added Master Jasper, improving the occasion. "Handsome is as handsome does!"

The girls did indeed present a great contrast, in

features and expression, as they stood side by side in the sunshine. Mabel was large for her age, well grown, plump as a partridge and straight as an arrow. Her black hair was naturally crimped to the very roots, and curled out from under the little muslin cap, which was bound round her head with a red ribbon, in dozens of crisp little rings. Her complexion, of cherries and milk, was heightened by her walk, and her blue eyes were shaded by black lashes, which heightened their brilliancy wonderfully. Altogether she was as handsome a girl as one would see in a summer's day. If there was any drawback to this beauty, it was that the chin was a trifle too heavy, the lips had something of a scornful curl, and the head was set up with a certain expression of self-assurance.

Isabel certainly presented a great contrast to her companion. She was as old as Mabel; but she was nearly a head shorter, and slight in proportion, her hands and feet being especially delicate. Her fair hair was as smooth and straight as floss silk, while her eyebrows were several shades darker, and her gray eyes were shaded by lashes as long and thick as Mabel's own. Her features were regular and delicate; but the chief peculiarity of her face was the total absence of color. Only her lips had a slight tinge of healthy red. Her general expression was one of sorrowful, brooding thoughtfulness, lighted up now and then by a lovely smile.

"Come here a moment, Mabel," called Dame Winne, from the dairy. "I want you to leave this cream cheese and this pot of honey for schoolmistress as you go past the stone cottage, with my duty to her. And Mabel, my dear, you will be kind and good to Isabel, will you not? Remember 'tis a poor orphan maid, with no one to care for her but strangers, and a weakly little thing, to boot, not strong and well grown like thee and thy mates. Help her in her lessons and her work, and don't let her be shamed before the others, for I dare say she is backward, poor thing! though she reads like parson himself. You will be good to her, will you not?"

"Indeed I will try, Aunt Bell," replied Mabel, at once flattered and softened by the stranger's being put under her protection. "But who is she?"

"She is the grandchild of my only sister, who married and went to live away in Worcestershire," replied the dame. "Word came to Jasper that Isabel's mother was dead, and she was alone in the wide world, and like to come to trouble among strangers. So as the Lord has given us plenty of this world's goods, and no children to inherit them, why there seemed a distinct call to us to take this poor maid home and care for her. Poor dear! I fear she will not be a care to us very long, unless she gains more strength."

"I dare say she will be better for the change!" said Mabel, taking the little basket, which the dame had been packing while she was talking. "Come, Isabel, we will go."

It was not without a little inward trepidation that Mabel met the schoolmistress. She was conscious that she had not behaved very well. But the mistress greeted her with all her usual kindness, and bade the girls go on to the school-house, while she put away her treasures. Mabel's heart was lightened, and she felt prepared to be very gracious to the stranger.

"How lame you are!" said she, slackening her steps as she saw that Isabel had some trouble in keeping up with her. "Were you always so?"

"No!" replied Isabel. "I could walk as well as any one a year ago; but I fell off the bridge, and I have never walked well since. It does not hurt me unless I walk very fast."

"We need not be in a hurry! No one will go till mistress comes."

"What are those tall chimneys!" asked Isabel, presently, pointing to some fantastically-ornamented chimneys which peered above the thick woods.

"That is Corby-End, where Captain Corbet lived," replied Mabel. "He took all his family away to London after the troubles a year or so ago."

"What troubles?" asked Isabel.

"Why, don't you know? Oh, I forgot, you are a stranger. Well, they said Madam Corbet was a witch. There was a family named Drum lived down at the end of the lane, and the boy pretended—so some said—to be bewitched, and both he and his mother both declared it was Madam Corbet who did the mischief. So some of the village folks rose on her, and would have drowned her, for aught I know, only little Jack Brown ran down to the Cove, and fetched up the fishermen and sailors, who all worshipped the captain and his lady; and they beat off the villagers, and carried off the lady to her own house, where some of them kept guard day and night till the captain came home. Jan Lee, Janey's father, was the chief among them, and thrashed Tom Drum till he owned that it was all a sham! Parson saved him at last, however, or I don't know but Jan would have killed the boy!"

"And did parson believe that he was bewitched?" asked Isabel, whose dilated eyes and flushed cheeks—flushed only on one side, however—showed that she took a painful interest in the story.

"Not he! He has always been against the witch trials, and on one occasion went all the way to Exeter to save a poor woman's life, who was tried there, only he was too late!" replied Mabel.

"He is a good man!" said Isabel. "I thought he looked like one this morning. Which is Janey Lee?"

"There she stands, holding her little twin sisters by the hand!" replied Mabel, pointing her out. "How she gets those little things up the steep path from the Cove every day in time for school is a wonder. She will not have much fun this afternoon if she has them to look after. Here comes mistress. Now we shall set out!"

The two schools—the boys and the girls, or "maids," as they were always called—were soon assembled on the fine sloping lawn, shaded here and there by large trees, and overlooked by the high terrace and towers of the great house. The Stantoun family had always taken to gardening, since one of their number had gone in the train of an am-bassador to Italy, as far back as the reign of Henry Eighth: and the garden and grounds at Stantoun Court compared favorably with those of great houses much nearer to the capital. The queen had heard of them, and had even pro-posed to make them a visit during the last years of her life; but the way was long, and traveling, especially in the west country, difficult and dangerous; and, fortunately perhaps for the family, the visit never took place. I say fortunately, for royal visits were expensive things, and made sad holes in the estates and purses of those favored by them.

All the other children had seen the marvels of Stantoun Court many times before, and cared for nothing but their games on the grass or under the trees; but to Isabel it seemed like a fairy land. She kept close to Mabel or to the mistress, not offering to share in the many plays,—for which, indeed, her lameness, to some extent disqualified her,—but contented herself with looking about her, now and then asking a question concerning some flower or shrub, or the statues which adorned the terrace.

"And what is that?" she asked, half shrinking from a grotesque figure, "with the lower limbs of a goat, and holding in his hand a pipe?"

"That is an image of some heathen god," replied Mabel: "so I have heard, at least. To my thinking, it looks like the author of evil himself."

"He looks good-natured, though, withal!" said Isabel, venturing to approach nearer. "He looks lovingly at his pipe, as if he could make sweet music on it. But, Mabel, is it right to have images of heathen gods?"

"I never thought of that!" said Mabel, considering. "I suppose so, or such great people would not have them."

Isabel shook her head at this argument. "Just think what wicked things even kings have done sometimes,—the kings in the Bible, and bloody Queen Mary: yes, and even later than that!" added Isabel.

"But you know they only keep the images for show—not to worship them," said Mabel. "Perhaps that makes all the difference. We will ask the mistress some day. Here comes Cicely, running, well, sis?"

"We want all the big girls to come and play at 'Thread the needle!'"answered Cicely, almost breathless. "Come away, directly."

"Isabel cannot run, you know," said Mabel, "and she won't like being left alone in this strange place."

"Oh, never mind me! I will go and sit by the mistress, under the tree," said Isabel. "Do go, Mabel; I am sure they want you!"

"Well, if you don't mind! But where is Janey Lee?" asked Mabel, as they drew nearer to the many groups. "She is the best runner of all!"

"Yonder she is under the tree, with the twins," replied Cicely. "She will have no fun at all, as I see, for the poor little things are so scared at the strange place that she cannot leave them."

"What a shame!" said Mabel, as she joined the game. Isabel slipped away, and presently Jane Lee came running up and took her place in the line.

"Why, Janey, how did you get away," asked Cicely.

"Oh, Mabel's cousin Isabel has got the twins," replied Janey. "She came round and begged me to go and play while she took care of the children. And, would you believe it? the little things went to her at once, though they are so shy with strangers. I would not have let her sit still with them, only she said she was lame, and it tired her to walk about."

When they had tired themselves out at play, and the servants from the great house were seen to be preparing the tables for the feast, Mabel and Janey went in search of Isabel. They found her with one of the twins on her lap, and a dozen more little ones clustered round her knees, all listening intently to the tale she was telling them.

"If she has not got the whole first class!" said Mabel.

"And a good thing for them, too, poor little dears!"

returned Janey. "Does she not look lovely?—only so very white, like the marble angels on Lady Rosamond's tomb. Well, maids, are you hearing a nice story?"

"Oh yes; such a nice time!" answered one of the twins. "Isabel is telling us such a pretty tale! Please don't talk, Janey! Well, Isabel, and so the poor little babies—"

"Well, I declare! I seem to be quite cut out!" said Janey, good-humoredly. "I suppose I may listen!"

"Of course, if you like!" said Isabel; but she seemed rather embarrassed, as if she were shy of talking before those of her own age.

"No, no, don't!" said Annie Hulton. "You put her out, and we want her all ourselves!"

"Come, then, Mabel, we will bestow ourselves else-where!" said Jane, putting her arm through Mabel's to draw her away. Then, as they passed out of hearing, "Did you ever see any thing like it?" "She has won all their hearts already!"

"I think she takes a good deal on herself for a stranger!" said Mabel, looking not very well pleased.

"I am sure it is very kind in her, Mabel!"

"It may be kind enough; but it is not very becoming, to my mind!" returned Mabel.

"Jealous, Mabel?"

"No, I am not jealous! Why should I be jealous, and of a chit like her?"

"Why, indeed?"

"But I don't like to see a stranger so forward!" contin-ued Mabel, with still more asperity; "and I don't think you need take her part against me, Janey. But every new broom sweeps clean with you."

Janey made no answer, well knowing, by experience, that to do so would be only to draw upon herself the weight of Mabel's displeasure. She endeavored to change the subject.

"See, there is the mistress, sitting quite alone on the stone seat. Let us go and speak to her."

Mabel assented, and they turned towards the great tree.

"Well, Mabel, how are you enjoying yourself?" asked the mistress, kindly.

"Pretty well!" replied Mabel; but there was no enjoyment in her tone.

"Your cousin seems to have found business for herself!" said the mistress, looking towards the place where Isabel still sat surrounded by the little ones. She had improvised a doll for them, by dressing up a dry knot of wood in her handkerchief, and they were in the midst of a great game of housekeeping. Isabel looked more animated, more like a live child and less like a marble statue, than Elizabeth had yet seen her, as she sat in the midst of her little flock, now and then putting in a word, or raising a warning finger as the frolic seemed likely to pass beyond due bounds.

"I wish she would not call Isabel my cousin!" was Mabel's thought; but she only said, "Yes, she seems to like children."

"It must be quite a relief to you, Jane, to have the twins taken off your hands!" continued the mistress.

"Yes, indeed!" replied Jane, heartily. "I should not have been able to play at all if Isabel had not coaxed them so cleverly, for they are so shy, they will never go near a stranger. Mother was hardly willing to let them come; but I could not bear to disappoint the poor little things."

"It will be a comfort to you, Mabel, if Isabel does take to the 'babes!'" said the mistress. "It will take a good deal off your hands."

"Yes!" said Mabel, again; "but I do not mind the trouble of the little ones." Then, as she saw the penetrating eye of the mistress fixed upon her, she said, hastily, as if to change the subject,—

"Mistress, is it wrong to have images of heathen gods?"

"No, if they are only kept for ornament, and not to be worshipped," replied the mistress. "What made you think of that?"

"Isabel and I were looking at the image with the goat's legs, and talking about it, and she thought it was wrong," replied Mabel. "I told her that I thought my lord would not have them if it was wrong; but she said that was nothing, and that great people did wrong just as much as others."

"Isabel should not sit in judgment upon her betters!" said the mistress. "However, she is right so far as this, that if a thing be wrong, the fact of ever so many great people's doing it does not make it right."

Mabel had not perhaps deliberately intended to misrepresent her cousin's words; but she was not in her heart displeased to see that the mistress had taken up a false impression, and she did nothing to remove it. With renewed good-humor she chatted on about various matters, till the bell summoned the guests to the tables.

"Come, Mabel!" said Janey, "let us go and find Isabel. It would not be fair to let her tend baby all afternoon: and you know she is a stranger."

"She does not seem to feel very much like one!" said Mabel. "I dare say she can take care of herself!" And she turned in a different direction. The little ones meantime had run to seek their sisters and friends, and Isabel was left sitting alone under the tree. She had supposed that Mabel would of course come for her, and she was too shy to go forward by herself; so she was left alone, while the girls and boys ranged themselves along the sides of the tables, and, with folded hands, waited for the pastor to come and say grace. The doctor took his place at the head of the board. The grace was repeated, and then taken up and sung by the children.

The servants from the great house, assisted by some of the older exschool-girls from the village, helped the guests liberally to currant-buns and mugs of sweet milk, and still nobody missed the little stranger, who sat under the tree, feeling very forlorn and very undecided as to what she ought to do. The mistress was helping the housekeeper with the cakes and milk, and if she thought of Isabel at all, she supposed, of course, that she was un-der Mabel's protection.

At last there was a buzzing whisper of "My lady!" "Here is my lady coming!" and Lady Stantoun, leaning upon the arm of the doctor, and followed by the master and mistress, made the circuit of the tables, speaking a kind word to each child as she passed. When she reached the end of the row of girls, she paused and turned round to the mistress.

"Doctor Parnell, tells me that there is a new girl, Mistress Ellenwood,—a niece or grandchild of Master Jasper Winne,—which is she? I think I know all these faces!"

Mistress Ellenwood looked down the long lane; but no black dress was to be seen.

"Why, Mabel, where is your cousin?"

"I don't know!" replied Mabel, trying to speak as usu-al, but feeling the burning color rush into her cheeks. "I thought she was with the little ones!"

Mistress Ellenwood gave Mabel a look which made her feel very small indeed.

"Her place was with you, as you very well know! Keep your seat," she said, as Mabel, muttering some excuse, rose from her place. "I will go and find her myself."

"Please, mistress, she is under the oak tree!" whis-pered little Patience. "I see her black frock."

"Why, my poor maid! why do you sit here alone?" said the mistress, taking the hand of Isabel, and leading her to the table. "Did no one come for you?"

"No, madam; but please mistress, I don't mind. I would rather go home!"

"But that would not do at all!" said the mistress. "My lady has asked for you, and you must come to her."

Isabel said no more, but suffered herself to be led to my lady, to whom she made her little courtesy.

"Why, my poor maid! did every one overlook you, and you a stranger?" said Lady Stantoun, kindly. "Girls, that was not right. Isabel,—that is your name is it not?" Isabel curtsied again. "Isabel will have but a poor notion of our west country manners."

The girls stood far too much in awe of my lady for any of them to venture to make a reply or an excuse; but they looked at each other, and then at Mabel, who, almost choking with shame and anger, half wished that she might sink into the ground and be seen no more.

"But I dare say it was a mistake, and that was all!" continued my lady, good-humoredly. "Never mind! Here is a place for you, by Cicely, who will take good care of you, I am sure; will you not, Cicely?"

"Oh, yes, my lady!" replied Cicely, blushing with pleasure at being thus singled out by Lady Stantoun.

The girls eagerly made room for Isabel, and whispered to her not to mind.

"And so you are come to live at the Red House?" continued Lady Stantoun, again addressing Isabel. "I think I have seen your mother, when we were both girls. Did she come home with you?"

"No, my lady," replied Isabel, the hectic flush mounting into her cheek. "My mother is dead, and my father too!" she added, sadly.

"Poor child! You are young to be left thus alone in the world; but I doubt not you will a find a happy home with Master Jasper and his good dame. You must be a dutiful child to them, and a good girl in school, and thus I hope you may be happy!"

Isabel looked up with beaming eyes and the sudden pathetic smile which made her face for the moment almost angelic. Lady Stantoun was a kind-hearted woman, and apt to follow her impulses, which, to do her justice, were usually good ones. She stooped and kissed the upturned face, and there were tears in her own eyes.

"There, be a good maid!" said she, and again taking the arm of the doctor, she walked on towards the boys' table.

All this did not tend to calm Mabel's excited feelings.

She knew that she had done wrong, that she had neglected her duty as head girl of the school, in not attending to Isabel, and that she had been willfully unkind to the orphan stranger. But it was not the wrongdoing which most afflicted her. The mistress, whom she almost worshipped, was seriously displeased with her, and my lady, though she had not blamed her, and had spoken to her by name as usual, had yet not distinguished her by any particular notice, while she had talked with and even kissed this insignificant chit, whom she had never seen before. Then her schoolmates evidently thought her to blame, from the glances they cast at her. And all was the fault of that new comer,—that interloper, who had arrived from no one knew where, to steal from her that what she most valued. From that hour a feeling of bitter envy and hatred sprang up in Mabel's mind towards her cousin. It was but a small shoot to begin with, and a vigorous effort might doubtless have crushed it in the bud; but no such effort was made. On the contrary, Mabel cherished the "bitter root," which was destined to grow and bear fruit by which her life was poisoned.

When the feast was over, the games were renewed with fresh spirit; but Mabel would join in none of them. She stood under the trees, looking on, now at the dancers on the turf, now at the little ones who had again claimed Isabel, while higher and higher in her heart swelled the tide of shame and anger. To be disgraced, and on the feast-day, of all days in the year! In vain did the girls beg her to play; in vain did my lady herself speak to her, and ask if she were not well; in vain did Isabel, breaking away from the children, come to her side and try to draw her into conversation. Mabel met her cousin's timid advances either with contemptuous smiles or in total silence, and persisted in being sullen and alone.

When the children were dismissed, at the school-room door, Mabel lingered a little behind, expecting she hardly knew what. Surely the mistress would not let her go without speaking to her! Elizabeth sat down in the porch, and called Mabel to her.

"Mabel!" said she. "What has been the matter today?"

Mabel hung her head, and said nothing.

"What has ailed you, to make you act so strangely and improperly? You have spoiled your own pleasure, and you have neglected your duty as head girl of the school, which was to attend to the new scholars,—to say nothing of your duty to your cousin. Why was this?"

Mabel had never been seriously reproved by the mistress before. She could not endure blame from any one, least of all from those whom she loved. She raised her head proudly, and her eyes flashed.

"I do not know why I am to be blamed for all!" said she. "I thought Isabel was with the little ones, as she had been all the afternoon. Besides, she is not a baby. She might have come to the table herself well enough!"

"You know that she is a stranger, and would not know what to do," replied the mistress. "You know that it is part of your duty to see that all the girls are in their places at such times, and, as I said before, you are specially bound to attend to strangers. Isabel's being 'a baby' or not has nothing to do with the matter. You have done wrong, Mabel, and the only proper way for you is to acknowledge it, and beg pardon."

Mabel was silent.

"Come, Mabel! Let me see that you can conquer yourself. Have you not done wrong?"

"I don't know that I have done any thing!" said Mabel, her temper now fully aroused, for the first time in the mistress's presence. "If you think that I do not do my duty, you may put some one else in my place."

The moment the words were spoken, Mabel wished them unsaid. If they had been addressed to her mother, or to any former mistress of the school, they would have insured her a sound whipping,—for the birch tree was esteemed a sovereign cure for perverseness in those days, and many an older girl than Mabel had tasted the discipline of the rod. But Elizabeth was not fond of corporal punishment, and she loved Mabel. She sat for a moment in silence.

"Very well, Mabel!" said she. "I shall say no more to you. You know very well what your words and your conduct might bring upon you; but I wish to save you from your own folly, if possible. I give you till Saturday morning to consider whether you will submit and ask pardon or not. If by that time you have not obeyed me, I shall not be able to save you from merited disgrace. But until you do your duty, you must not presume to speak to me!" So saying, she turned into the school-house and shut the door, and Mabel walked homeward, more miserable than she had ever been in all her life before.

CHAPTER III

THE LACE-MAKING

IT was with a heavy heart that Mabel prepared to go to school the next morning. An unpleasant alternative lay before her. Either she must humble herself, and beg mistress's pardon, or she must allow all the girls to see that she was in disgrace. She must have her contumacy reported to "parson," and to Lady Stantoun, and most likely be dismissed from the school, for no open rebellion was to be tolerated for a moment in Lady Rosamond's school. Should she be dismissed, she would be disgraced for life. Nobody would take her part, not even her own parents, for her mother, though she could hardly read herself, was very anxious to have her daughter "book-learned," and her father was a man of stern, uncompromising character, who never overlooked an offence in child or in servant. It was a hard trial; but the more she thought of it, the more clearly she saw that she had no escape. With a swollen heart she got ready for school, and prepared to beg the mistress's pardon. If she had done so from a sense of duty, if she had consented to own herself, in the first place, that she had been wrong, all might have been well. But this was not the case. She still persisted in considering herself the injured person, and Isabel as the cause of her disgrace. There was no sincerity, no reality in the proceedings. Mabel asked pardon not because she was sorry, but because she dared not do otherwise, and the consequence was that the humiliation did her more harm than good. She felt as though she should choke, as she stood at the gate of the stone cottage, waiting for the mistress to make her appearance, and when she did make an effort to speak, the words hardly came forth at her bidding. They were said, however, and the mistress received them in a kindly spirit.

"Very well, Mabel! I shall say no more about the matter, and I trust I shall never again have occasion to reprove you. But remember, sweet-heart, that action speaks louder than words. Let me see by your conduct that you are sorry for your unkindness towards poor Isabel, who certainly can have done nothing to offend you seriously in the short time that you have known her."

"The mistress thinks that Isabel is better than I am!" was Mabel's first thought. It was an unjust one. Elizabeth never made up her mind hastily, and though pleased with what she had seen of Isabel, she had formed no decided opinion about the little girl. Mabel said little more until they reached the schoolhouse; but when Isabel came, rather timidly, to meet her, she constrained herself to answer her cousin's greeting with tolerable cordiality.

Isabel found her first school-days rather less trying than she expected. The girls were disposed to be kind to her, though they laughed among themselves at her timidity, and sometimes, when out of the mistress's sight, teased her with rough play. Mistress Ellenwood was wise and considerate, and gave her time to become used to the ways of the school; and she had already a strong party among the little ones: with them she was at her ease. She told them tales without end, taught them little verses and amusing ditties, and was once heard even to laugh merrily at Grace Lee's efforts to imitate on her fat fingers the traditional "flock of black-birds!"

"Please, Mabel, untie this knot for me and take up my stitches!" said Patience Penbuthy, one noon-time. "Puss has had my work and pulled it all to pieces; and now there she sits in the window, and looks as innocent as cream cheese!" added Patience, in an aggrieved voice, as she looked at the cat, who certainly showed no signs of a guilty conscience, as she sat watching her face in the window. Puss was an ancient inhabitant of the school-room, and was certainly old enough to know better; nevertheless, she was every now and then taken with a fit of "gamesomeness," as the girls said, and played many pranks very unbecoming to her years and station.

"What made you leave your work in the way of the cat? you tiresome little thing!" said Mabel, as she took the entangled work.

"It was on my seat, and she jumped up and got it. It wasn't half fair," replied Patience, just ready to cry at the mingled remembrance of her disordered work and the un-kindness of pussy.

"What a mess you have made of it!" said Mabel, not in a very good humor at being hindered herself. "I can do nothing with it, Patience!" she added, after a brief exami-nation, and two or three impatient jerks at the yarn. "You must pull it out up to here,"—marking the place,—"and then take up the stitches, or get one of the girls to take them up for you."

"Oh, dear!" said the poor child, beginning to cry,—"to lose all that work! I shall not get my socks done this week, and Saturday is baby's birthday. Please, Mabel, do try!" said she, imploringly.

"I tell you nothing can be done. The work is spoiled," returned Mabel, angrily, and giving the child a push. "Go and pull it out directly."

"Let me see!" said a gentle voice, as Patience turned away, drowned in tears, and Isabel took the work out of her hands and carried it to the window. Patience stood by in breathless admiration, as Isabel with patient dexterity pulled through and picked up the disordered stitches.

"There!" said Isabel, as she returned the work to its owner. "It is all right now! Be careful another time, and put your work in the basket, and then puss will not find it. She is only a dumb beast, and knows no better; but little girls do, and so it is naughty to be careless."

The little one received the lecture with all due humility, promised to be good, and, putting up her mouth for a kiss, she skipped away as happy as a lark. But Isabel had unwittingly got herself into trouble. Mabel's position as head girl gave her some authority over the little ones, and of this she had lately become very jealous. Isabel had interfered with her prerogative,—so she said to herself, in excuse for her anger; and what wounded her still more, Isabel had accomplished a task which she had pronounced impossible. Mabel's familiar evil spirit was roused in a moment.

"Poor Patience!" said Isabel, as she resumed her seat. "She thinks her friend puss very cruel to use her so."

"Patience, come here!" called Mabel, sharply, without answering Isabel. "Nay, bring your work!" she added. As the little girl unwillingly approached, she snatched the knitting out of her hands, pulled out the needles with a jerk, and raveling out two or three yards of yarn, she gave it back to her.

"Now go and do as I bade you, you naughty little thing! As for you, Isabel, I will thank you to mind your own business. If you meddle so again, I will tell the mistress, and see what she will say!"

Isabel looked at her in utter amazement.

"Why, Mabel, I did not mean—"

"Oh, you never do mean, of course! But I will have you know that I will have no meddling by you, or anybody! Patience, do as I tell you, this minute."

Patience was a passionate little thing, and the change from hope to despair was too much for her to endure. She threw the work down on the floor and burst into a passionate fit of crying.

"I won't touch it, that I won't! You are a mean, hateful thing, Mabel Winne, to serve me so. I will never come to you again, and I will tell the mistress—that I will! I wish Isabel was head of the school, and not you!"

Mabel's temper was now fully aroused. She took

Patience by the arm, and shook her soundly, ending by a severe slap.

"I will teach you to mind me!" she said, between her teeth, as she tightened her grasp on the little arm. "Pick up your work this minute, or I will pull every stitch of it out. Pick it up this moment!"

Patience screamed with fright and pain so loudly that she was heard outside the building, where the children were at play, and Cicely, her cousin, came running in, followed by two or three of the older girls.

"Patience, what is the matter?" exclaimed Cicely. "Mabel, you just let her alone!"

"She pulled out all my work, and shook me and beat me!" sobbed Patience; and as Mabel released her arm she held it up, sobbing, to show the marks of fingers on it. Then she picked up her knitting and burst into fresh sobs, as she saw its deplorable condition.

"For shame, Mabel, to use the child so!" said Cicely, warmly. "What has she done to be so treated?"

"That is none of your business, Cicely," returned Mabel. "Patience was very naughty, and Isabel took her part against me, and has made all this fuss. If she had minded her own business, nothing would have been the matter. As for Patience, she shall pull out her work herself, or I will do it for her."

"You shall not touch her work, nor her either!" retorted Cicely, who was very fond of her cousin, and had also a temper of her own. "Look at her poor arm, all black and blue now. You ought to be ashamed, Mabel, that you ought, and I will tell mistress;—see if I don't."

"What does all this mean?" asked a voice behind the group, and the mistress herself came in. There was silence in an instant, and Mabel began to look rather ashamed of herself.

"What are you crying for, Patience, and why do you rub your arm so?" asked the mistress, of the still sobbing child. "Have you hurt yourself?"

"Mabel hurt me!" said Patience, between her sobs, "and she has spoiled my work, after Isabel put it to rights for me; and now I shall not get it done in time for baby's birthday!"

"Mabel, did you hurt the child's arm like this?" asked the mistress, in astonishment, as she looked at the already swollen and discolored arm, which Patience could hardly move. "What were you thinking of, to do such a thing?"

"I should not have touched her at all if Isabel had not meddled!" said Mabel, sullenly. "She dropped her stitches and spoiled her work, and she was very naughty about it, and so I told her that she must pull it out and do it over. Then Isabel interfered, and said she would do it for her, and she took the work away from her and put it to rights."

"Well!" said the mistress, as Mabel paused,—"what then?"

"Then Patience was going away, and I called her and pulled the needles out myself, and told her she should do as I bid her. Then she threw down her work and screamed, and I shook her. If Isabel had minded her own business there would have been no trouble at all!"

"Now, Isabel, let me hear your story!" said the mistress, turning to her.

"I did not mean to interfere," said Isabel, timidly, but in a simple, straightforward manner. "I understood Mabel to say that the work could not be put to rights at all, so I thought, as it was to be pulled out any way, there would be no harm in trying what I could do. I did not mean to meddle between Mabel and Patience, and I did not know that she told Patience to pull out the work as a punishment, but only because she thought it could not be put in order without."

"That was what Mabel said!" interposed Patience; "she said nobody could pick up the stitches."

The mistress could not repress a smile. She understood Mabel far better than Mabel did herself.

"Well, well!" said she. "Let us have no more quarrelling. Mabel, you were wrong to be so harsh with the child, and Patience must be more careful another time. Give me your work! Cicely, take the child out to the well, and bind some cool, wet plantain leaves upon her arm. Go out all the rest except Mabel and Isabel, and shut the door!"

The mistress said nothing till she had taken up all the stitches upon the unlucky sock. Then she said,—

"Tell me the truth, now, Mabel! Did you, in the first place, tell Patience to pull out her work because she was naughty or because you thought there was no other way?"

Mabel, with all her faults, was truthful. She would not tell a falsehood,—at least not unless she was in a passion. She hesitated a moment, and then said,—

"I thought it was spoiled. I thought it would have to be pulled out at any rate."

"Then that was the reason, and not because she had been naughty?"

"Yes, please, mistress!"

"Did you understand it so, Isabel?"

"Yes, please, mistress! I should not have touched it else. I am very sorry!"

"I do not see in that case that you were to blame. There was no harm, but only kindness, in your helping the child, so long as you did not take her part against Mabel. Now so, I wish to talk to Mabel alone."

"Mabel, I think you have been wrong!" said the mistress, as soon as the door was shut, "You have abused your authority. I have said before this that I would have no striking or shaking of little girls by great girls. You have hurt the child seriously."

"I thought I ought to make her mind!" said Mabel. "I did not mean to hurt her so, but I was angry!"

"I know you were, and it is of that I wish to speak. Why were you angry: because Patience disobeyed you, or because Isabel did something that you could not? Tell me honestly, Mabel, was not the latter the true reason?"

Mabel knew well enough that it was, but she was too proud to own it. "I don't think she need have meddled!" she said.

"But it appears that she did not do so. There was no question of authority in the case. You could not do what Patience asked, and Isabel did it,—that was all. Then, when she had relieved the child of her trouble, you took the work and pulled it out. Was that right? Would you like to be served so? The other day when I could not open the gate for Dame Hollis, you came and opened it directly! Suppose I had slammed the gate to again, and told the old woman to open it for herself! What would you have thought of me?"

Mabel blushed crimson.

"But Patience *was* naughty. She stamped and screamed, and declared that she would not do it!"

"I dare say she was! But that was after you pulled out her work, was it not?"

Mabel admitted it.

"Do you not think she had some provocation, Mabel? Suppose any one had served your work so! What would you have said?"

"You are very wrong, Mabel!" said the mistress, after a few minutes' silence. "You have abused your authority, you have injured your influence, and disobeyed me, and you are committing the additional fault of laying all the blame upon your cousin, whose only error, if error there was at all, was one of judgment. Suppose she had been unable to do the work, and you had done it, do you think Isabel would have the right to be angry?"

"That is different!" said Mabel. "Isabel is not head girl."

"But I do not learn from your own account that your being head girl had any thing to do with the matter. Now, Mabel, my dear child, do not be obstinate and willful," added the mistress, affectionately. "Strive earnestly to conquer yourself, and do what is right,—what your Savior would approve!" she added, in a lower tone. "Think if he had been here and beheld you,—as he does behold every thought of your heart,—what he would have thought of you?"

"I was wrong to hurt Patience!" said Mabel, after a little pause, "but I did not mean to. It was my temper."

Elizabeth smiled.

"You speak of your temper as if it were something apart from yourself,—some wild beast or surly dog! Pray, who is responsible for your temper?"

"It is my natural disposition!" said Mabel. "I cannot help it!"

"Take care, my child! Do not deceive yourself in this matter. If you cannot help it, how is it that God will call you to account for it, as he surely will, unless you learn to govern it? The truth is, Mabel, you have not tried to overcome this fault. You hardly think of it as a fault, and the few efforts you have made have been in your own strength. I hardly know where it will lead you, unless you try to get the better of it.

"There is another thing which I have been sorry to see in you!" continued the mistress, "but I have no time to talk about it now. I believe it lay at the root of all the trouble this morning. If you think about the matter, I am persuaded that you will discover it for yourself. But, Mabel, remember this, you *cannot* conquer yourself!"

"I *can* conquer myself, and I will!" said Mabel, proudly, to herself. "She shall see that I can!"

"Here is your work, Patience!" said the mistress, as the children came in. "I have knit it up for you past the bad place, so that you can easily finish it. Mabel is sorry that she hurt your arm, and I think you are sorry for stamping and screaming. So kiss and be friends again!"

"Please, it was not Isabel's fault!" said Patience.

"Nobody blames Isabel!" replied the mistress, smiling at the little girl's resolute championship of her friend. "Come, now, do as I bid you, and let us hear no more of the matter."

For some days every thing went on quietly between Mabel and Isabel. Indeed Mabel was unusually gracious to her cousin, as if to make up for her injustice, though she did not go so far as to acknowledge in words that she was wrong; and she bestowed an extra amount of petting and seed-cakes upon Patience, whose discolored arm she could not see without an acute pang of mortification. Mabel was determined to show that she *could* conquer herself, and she succeeded so far as the outside was concerned.

But Mabel had begun at the wrong end. It is possible in weeding a garden to make it look nicely without much trouble. You may cut off the tops of the weeds, and rake over the beds neatly, and for a while feel very well satisfied with the work; but your satisfaction will not last long. The first warm sun or the first heavy rain—it does not matter which—will bring all the weeds up again as strong as ever. So it was with Mabel's reformation. She had indeed cut off the tops; but the "bitter root" was still there, ready on the first encouragement to send forth its shoots more strong than ever.

About this time a new kind of work was introduced into Lady Rosamond's school. Lady Stantoun had come from a part of the county where lace-making had been practiced for a long time, and proved profitable to those engaged in it, and she was desirous that the girls of the village should learn to make lace. She had consulted the mistress about the matter. Elizabeth was pleased with the idea. She knew something of the art herself, and was glad to learn more of Mrs. Brewster, my lady's gentlewoman, who understood all the mysteries of lace-making. So, after two or three weeks of practice on her part, a dozen lace pillows were produced, and the twelve best workwomen in the school, including Mabel, Isabel, Cicely, and Janey Lee, were put into a class together to learn to make the famous Devonshire lace, which was what we now call Honiton.

It was a great honor, to be sure, but it was rather a troublesome one. The work was hard to understand, and harder to practice. The thread was like cobweb, Cicely declared, and one ought to be a spider to manage it; the bobbins on which it was wound seemed devotedly fond of each other's company, and twisted themselves together in a surprising manner, or the pins would mysteriously drop out of the holes in the parchment pattern, and then the work was all wrong. I am afraid to say how many skeins of thread were wasted or how many tears were shed during the first three weeks of the lace-making.

After that matters began to improve. Some pretty specimens were produced and commenced, and Lady Stantoun encouraged the workwomen by buying and wearing their laces. Moreover, she promised a prize to the one who at the end of six months should produce the best specimen of the manufacture.

Mabel had never been remarkably successful in any description of needlework. She lacked the patience and care requisite to excellence, and she was apt to give needle or flax an impatient pull at some critical point. But, as we have seen, Mabel had set out to conquer herself, and she took up her lace pillow with a determination to succeed. This, however, was not so easy. It was by far the most difficult and delicate work she had ever undertaken, demanding patience and close attention as well as dexterity. Try as she would, she could not catch the "knack" with which the mistress tossed her bobbins about, and made the knots come in their right places, and her threads were constantly entangled and broken. If she had been content to proceed slowly, she would no doubt have done better; but Mabel had unbounded confidence in her own powers, and she began with the idea that she was going to succeed directly, and stand at the head of the school in that as she did in other things. In vain did the mistress advise her to take time, and learn one step thoroughly before she went on to another.

"Mabel knew it all!" the girls said, and she was impatient to prove that she did so. The consequence was that at the end of three weeks' practice there was not one of the girls, except hopelessly dull Peggy Hollins,—who never learned any thing,—who did not succeed better than Mabel.

It was mortifying enough, no doubt; but what added the chief element of bitterness to her disappointment was the fact that while she was nearly at the foot of the lace-making class, Isabel was decidedly at the head. Her delicate, thin fingers seemed expressly made to bundle the slender threads, and Mistress Brewster declared, with admiration, that Isabel's eye and touch were as true as her own, and that some of her sprigs were as nice as if she had done them herself; and she, not very judiciously, perhaps, held Isabel up as a model to the whole class.

"Look at her work," said Mrs. Brewster, "how clean and neat it is! with no knots like yours, Cicely, and no loose places like yours, Mabel Winne. Why don't you take pattern by her?"

"Isabel does everything better than any one else,—except Janey, perhaps,"—said good-natured Cicely. "Janey's is *almost* as nice as Isabel's!"

"I am used to making nets; perhaps that may be the reason," said Janey.

"You are used to taking pains, which has something to do with it, and you are willing to be told the right way, which is more!" returned Mrs. Brewster, who had not been pleased with Mabel's manner, considering her altogether too forward and confident, and she now took the opportunity of administering a reproof. "Mabel, has far too good a conceit of herself to learn readily. You will have to go back to the beginning again, Mabel: there is no other way. Sit you down here with Peggy Hollins, and you, Janey, go to the head of the class, next to Isabel."

Poor Mabel! It was the greatest mortification of her life!—greater than that she had received at the school feast. It was with a swelling heart that she took her place next to poor Peggy; but she sent back the angry drops from her eyes with a brave effort, and took up her work again, determined not to show that she was mortified. Isabel looked far more distressed at her promotion than Mabel did at her degradation; but she was too timid, as Mabel was too proud, to make any objection.

When school was out, Isabel came round to where Mabel was sitting, brooding over her disgrace.

"Mabel!" said she, "I wish you would let me show you about the lace-making. Mistress Brewster is so quick, it is not easy to follow her, and I think you are rather near-sighted."

Mabel's first thought was to refuse the offered help, ungraciously enough. She recollected herself, however, and answered civilly,—

"I am sure you are very kind. I should be very glad to improve, but I don't believe I shall ever learn. I really believe I am bewitched!"

Isabel started at the word, as if she had been shot, and turned, as it seemed, a shade paler than she was before; but she recovered herself again, and took the pillow upon her lap, though Mabel saw that her fingers trembled at first. She almost forgot her vexation as she watched Isabel's nimble hands and followed her clear, simple directions.

"Now try!" said Isabel. "Tie the first knot slowly, till you learn it. Yes; that is right! Now, again! Don't you see now?"

Mabel thought she did, but when she tried again, she again failed. Tears of vexation started into her eyes.

"Oh, never mind! Don't cry, Mabel; please don't!" said Isabel. "You will learn it presently. See, this is the way! Try again!"

"That I will not!" exclaimed Mabel, her temper getting the better of her prudence. "I will never touch it again!"

"Oh, don't say so! Think how angry the mistress will be, and my lady. You are not half so slow as I was about learning the knitting stitch when my mother tried to teach it me, and I did learn it, after all. Try once more!"

"I tell you I will not touch it!" returned Mabel. "You may

enjoy your triumph, Mistress Isabel, and much good may it do you. Go on your own way, undermining me with my lady and with the mistress and the girls, as you have been doing ever since you came, and see what you will gain by it!"

"Why, Mabel!" said Isabel, perfectly amazed at the outbreak. "What have I done that you talk to me so?"

"You think I do not see through your deceitful arts!" continued Mabel, her temper rising, as usual, with indulgence. "Because you are so smooth and sly, and never say a word above your breath, you think nobody can understand you; but I know you. You may blind the eyes of the mistress, as clever as she is; and you may hoodwink my uncle and aunt by your acts,—poor old purblind souls as they are;—but you cannot bewitch me."

Again Isabel started painfully, and an expression of horror came over her face.

"Don't, Mabel; don't go on so!" she said, imploringly; "but tell me how I have displeased you. What have I done?"

"What have you done? Why did you manage to get me into disgrace at the school feast, the first thing? Why did you put in your word with Patience Penbuthy that day? Why did you contrive to get me into trouble with Mrs. Brewster, and send me to the bottom of the class? Before you came, I was every thing with Uncle Jasper and Aunt Bell. Now I am nothing. Before you came I was the favorite with the mistress, and my lady always noticed me. Now, whenever she comes it is, 'Where is my little Isabel?' Why did you come here at all?"

"Because I had no other place to go, Mabel," replied Isabel, with a quivering lip. "Because I was an orphan and had no home!"

"I wish you had been drowned in the river when you crossed the ferry," said Mabel, not heeding her cousin's mournful words. "I wish you were drowned for a witch, like Dame Brooks at Exeter!"

Isabel rose from her seat, and fixed on Mabel her large gray eyes, flashing with indignation, while the curious one-sided blush rose to her cheeks, and she seemed actually to grow taller.

"Mabel!" said she, in a low, thrilling voice, "those are wicked words, and you are a wicked girl to say them, and unless you repent of them you will surely be punished. I have never done harm to you or any one, and I never will; but remember what we read this morning about oppressing the stranger and the fatherless. Come, Mabel, do let us be friends!" she added, with winning tenderness in her tones. "I do love you, and I have so few friends! For your own sake, don't say such dreadful words!"

Mabel pushed away the proffered hand.

"Let me alone!" said she. "I want no friendship with you. You are a mischief-maker and a cheat,—a witch, too, for aught I know!" she added, remembering how Isabel had started at the word before. "You are my enemy, and I hate you!"

"If I *were* your enemy, Mabel, you ought not to hate me!" said Isabel; "but I am not! I have never done you the least harm, unless you call it harm to make the lace better than you, and that I cannot help. If you would only be patient, I could show you about it in a very little while!"

"I want none of your showing!" returned Mabel, "nor any thing else of you. You have been a torment to me, and have made me miserable ever since you came here, and I say again, I wish you had been drowned in the ferry before you ever came here, to set the mistress against me and rob me of all I love best."

Isabel turned away, and began to put on her cloak and hood to go home; nor did she answer one word more to the reproaches and insults Mabel poured upon her.

"Now go and tell the mistress all about it!" added Mabel, as Isabel opened the schoolhouse door. "That will be a fit ending to your performances."

"I shall not tell the mistress of you, Mabel!" replied Isabel, turning at the door, and looking at her. "I shall tell no one but God."

CHAPTER IV

THE SECRET GRIEF

MABEL went home with her heart burning with anger and mortification. She felt conscious that she had been mean and unjust to Isabel, at the very time Isabel was doing her best to help her, and, also, that though she had succeeded in hurting Isabel, she had not, after all, had the best of the encounter. Was this the result of her proud boast that she could conquer herself? It was all Isabel's fault! Mabel's outbreaks always were somebody else's fault, according to her own account of the matter. Somebody or something always provoked her!

"But I *will not* be beaten, and by her!" she thought, compressing her lips and stamping her foot. "The mistress does not care for me any more; but I will show her that I can be as good as her soft-spoken minions any day, ay, and as clever too, though she had all the witches in England to help her."

With this determination Mabel went to school the next day. She half hoped that Isabel would refuse to reply when she spoke to her; but Isabel answered just as usual, though she seemed more depressed and timid than ever, and her eyes looked swollen and heavy, as though she might have cried herself to sleep. Mabel took much pains with her lessons and with her work, and gained great commendation.

"Why, this is a great improvement, Mabel!" said the mistress. "This is the best you have done yet."

Mabel's head was raised proudly, and she glanced at Isabel; but Isabel seemed intent upon her work. The mistress passed along the class, commending or criticizing as the case required, till she came to Isabel.

"Why, Isabel, this is beautiful!—really beautiful!" she repeated, as she examined the work. "I do not think Mistress Brewster herself could have done it better. What is this?" she added, taking up a bit of paper which was pinned on Isabel's pillow. "Why, Isabel, is this your doing?"

Isabel looked up with a scared face, as though she expected to be blamed.

"Please, mistress, I was only trying to make up some patterns for myself," said she. "I picked the leaves last evening, and I thought they would make a pretty sprig. That was all!"

"There is no harm done, my maid! You need not look so frightened!" said the mistress, smiling. "I think your pattern is a very pretty one indeed. We will show it to Mistress Brewster, and if she thinks it is practicable, you shall try to make it yourself."

Isabel blushed and smiled, and Mabel felt a new pang of envy. Was she always to be eclipsed by this newcomer? When the class was dismissed at recess time, all the girls gathered round Isabel, to see the new pattern. It was really a pretty, spirited outline of a sprig of sweet-briar, and showed a great deal of talent in one who had never had the least instruction; but to Isabel's schoolmates, none of whom had ever in their lives thought of drawing any thing from nature, it seemed nothing less than marvelous.

"See the little notches in the edges of the leaves!" said one.

"And the thorns too, just like the real sweet-briar!" added another. "You must get the fairies to help you, Isabel."

"The witches, more likely!" said Mabel, remembering how Isabel had winced at the word. "Perhaps Isabel is a witch herself! Who knows!"

"Mabel, for shame!" said Janey Lee, warmly. "You have no right to say such things."

"She is only in joke!" said Isabel, forcing herself to speak, though her lips trembled.

"It is not a thing to say even in a joke!" returned Janey, gravely. "You might remember, Mabel, what things have happened here before now."

"You mean about Madam Corbet!" asked Annie Hutton. "But, Janey, some folks think she did not get half her desert, after all!"

"Some folks are fools!" was the contemptuous response of Janey Lee, who inherited all her father's loyalty to the Corbet family, as well as his determined Sadducism on the subject of witches.

"The king believes in witches, any way!" said Annie, with the air of one who brings forward a knock-down argument. "He wrote a book about it, for Doctor Matthew told my father so."

"The king is a Solomon, of course: everybody knows that!" said Janey, in a tone of no great respect. Her father and grandfather had been "old sailors of the queen's," and had no special regard for the reigning monarch.

"And there are witches in the Bible too!" continued Annie. "You can't deny that, Janey Lee!"

"A great many things happened in Bible times which don't happen now!" said Janey. "Angels used to come down to earth; but we do not see them in these days,—not very often."

"And if we do, we do not know them for angels till they are gone!" murmured Isabel. "Janey, are you going now? If you are, I will walk with you. Aunt Bell said I was to go down to the Cove, and carry some posset and marmalet to Faith Dean, and I don't like to go down the cliff alone. Aunt Bell said you would show me the way, and we will stop at our house for the basket."

"Oh, how nice!" exclaimed Janey. "The babes will be as happy as kitlings! Do you hear that, maids? Isabel is going home with us!"

"Oh, how fine that will be!" exclaimed little Dolly,

while Grace, Isabel's special pet, could express her delight
in no other way than by getting hold of Isabel's hand and
kissing and fondling it.

"Do you really think she is a witch, Mabel?" asked
Peggy Hollins, after Isabel had gone. Peggy was the dunce
of the school, disliked by all her mates, and by none more
than Mabel, for her awkward and untidy ways, which
were constantly making trouble for herself and others. At
another time, Mabel would have repelled her advances;
but her heart was full of evil passions, striving for a vent,
and she answered with seeming carelessness, but real
malice,—

"Like enough, for aught I know. There have been
younger witches than she, if all tales be true."

The moment Mabel had spoken the words she wished
them unsaid. She knew what a gossiping creature Peggy
was, ready to carry any sort of tale from one end of the
village to the other. She knew what fearful consequences
might result from an accusation or even a suspicion of
witchcraft. Conscience told her that her words had been
prompted by the desire to be revenged upon Isabel,—not
for any injury, but because Isabel had done something
which she could not. Mabel's conscience had been awak-
ened, and in some degree educated, under Elizabeth
Ellenwood's careful teaching. She had a strong sense of
right and wrong, and she had read her Bible enough to
have some idea of the holiness of God and of his Son. She
admired and remembered the character of her Savior,
and sometimes wished that she were like him. Nay, she
had gone so far as to determine more than once that she
would be like him. But she had not even made a beginning, because she had not felt herself a sinner. She had
her faults: that she confessed; but in her heart she did
not think them of much consequence. Her temper was
her "natural disposition," and then people were "always
provoking her!" She knew she was apt to be domineer-
ing; but had she not a right to be so? Her father was a

person of wealth and consequence; and was she not the
head girl in Lady Rosamond's school, and acknowledged
its best scholar, at least before this interloper came to rob
her of her right? No; though Mabel confessed herself a
miserable sinner every Sunday of her life, she did not in
her heart think herself so. This last indulgence of malice
opened her eyes a little, and might have been—as sometimes happens with such falls—the beginning of better
things. Mabel had always prided herself on her gener-
osity. She was hasty, she said, sometimes, but at least
she was not spiteful, and she did not bear malice; but she
could not deny that here had been both spite and malice.
She even debated whether she should not tell Peggy that
she had spoken improperly, and that she must not repeat
or believe the words; but this would involve the confession
that she was in the wrong; and was she to humble herself
before stupid Peggy Hollins? "After all, it would only be
making the matter of consequence to say any more about
it!" she said to herself. "I dare say Peggy will forget it in
an hour, and there will be the end of the matter."

But Mabel's conscience would not be thus easily satisfied, and more than once during the evening did it make
its voice heard, only to be silenced by its possessor. Mabel
had lately said her prayers every night. Not that she particularly felt the need of any thing; but good people said
their prayers, and she was going to be good. This night,
however, for some reason which perhaps she could not
have explained, she omitted them altogether, thus laying
another weight upon her over-burdened conscience, and
giving her adversary an advantage over her. Poor Mabel!

"Please, Dame, let Isabel come to our house to supper!"
said Janey, as kind Dame Winne filled her hands and those
of the children with cakes. "I will come up the cliff with her,
and it will be light till long after eight o'clock. May she!"

"Surely, my maid, if she likes, and thy good mother
wishes to have her!" replied Dame Winne. "It will be a
nice change for her!"

Isabel had not been used to such steep ways as the path down the cliff, which many of my most fearless readers would think twice or thrice about before undertaking: and Janey expected to see her show some timidity; but she was mistaken. Isabel followed her down the bank as coolly as if she, like Janey, had gone over it twice a day ever since she could remember.

"Isabel is not afraid a bit!" said Grace, in admiration.

"What would hurt me?" asked Isabel, with her sad smile.

"You might fall and be killed!" said Grace, doubtfully.

"I am not afraid of being killed!" said Isabel: adding, in a lower tone, "being killed is not the worst thing which happens to people."

"But you must not look down,—not down there, Isabel," cried Janey, herself alarmed as, looking round, she perceived Isabel leaning forward and gazing curiously over the edge of the cliff. A small stream, which gave the hamlet its name of Freshwater Cove, here fell over the rocks into a deep dark pool beneath, called Dobby's pool. The water, after circling round its basin, found an outlet by some subterraneous channel among the rocks, and was lost to view, and it was popularly said that nothing that dropped into Dobby's pool was ever seen again. At very high tide the course of the current was reversed, and the sea-water poured into the basin with a hollow roaring sound, which, when unusually loud, was supposed to foretell a storm.

"You must not look into Dobby's pool, Isabel," repeated Janey, seeing that Isabel did not withdraw her gaze. "Every one who does so grows giddy, and if any one falls in, his body is never found again."

"Dobby gets them!" said little Grace, in an awestruck voice. "It would be dreadful, Isabel, if such a thing happened to you?"

"Hush, Gracy!" said Janey. "What did mistress say?"

"What *did* she say?" asked Isabel, withdrawing her

eyes, as it seemed with difficulty, from the dark whirling pool so far beneath.

"Tell her, Gracy!"

"She said we must not think about Dobby, nor about any evil spirit!" repeated the child. "She said we must think of our Lord, and the good angels he sends to care for us, and that even if one fell into the pool and was drowned, Dobby nor nothing else could keep the angels from carrying him to paradise, if he only loved God and prayed to him."

"That's my fine maid!" said Janey, to remember what mistress said. "Now, do you and Dolly keep behind us, and mind you don't slip in as you pass. Take heed, Isabel! The spray makes the rocks slippery."

"That was what the mistress said one day, when she found Peggy telling the little ones horrid stories,—stories about Dobby and all such things," continued Janey. "She gave Peggy a good lecture, and then she talked to us all about it. She said if we must think about spirits, it had better be about glorified spirits and angels than about devils and goblins."

"I think mistress is like an angel herself!" said Isabel.

"You might say so if you knew her as the poor sick folks do hereabout!" replied Janey, warmly. "There is no one she will not go to see,—not even poor Anne Styles at the Millheads," she added, lowering her voice, "though the village folks treated her like the dirt under their feet when she came back from Exeter. There was Tom Tripp, who died down here at the Cove. The mast fell on him and broke his back, and after the doctor said he could not live, his distress was awful to see. He had no pain: 'twas all his mind and conscience, and no one could comfort him. Parson was away to Exeter that time, and nobody knew what to do. Finally his sister went away up the cliff just at night, to see if the mistress could do any thing for them in their trouble, for Tom, though he was a rough, hard fellow, and would swear so that it would make your blood run cold, was a kind son and brother. 'Twas a cold, dark, rainy night, but mistress no sooner heard the tale than she put on her hood, and came away down the cliff to Tom's house,—there it stands yonder by the big stone; and they said she could hear him groan and cry all the way off here. She stayed there all night, and till daddy brought her into our house just to get a bite of something, before going up the cliff in the morning, and when she came away, Tom was as quiet as a lamb. He never complained all day, though his pains came on worse than ever, and father said he died at last just as peaceful as our little baby. Father ventured to ask him what mistress had done for him, and he said he would never forget Tom's face and voice as he answered, 'she made me to see and feel the goodness of God!'"

Janey paused, for the great tears were running down Isabel's cheeks, and her hands were clasped tightly together, while her face wore an expression which Janey could not understand.

"The goodness of God!" she murmured, "Oh, to see the goodness of God once more!"

"What ails Isabel?" asked Grace.

"Hush! Don't notice her!" whispered Janey, with instinctive tact. "There, run along to mother."

When Janey turned round, Isabel was still standing in the same place, and it was not till Janey touched her that she roused herself.

"What have I said?" she exclaimed, starting.

"Nothing, dear!" replied Janey, "only, dear Isabel, I am sure I didn't mean to make you cry!"

"You didn't!" said Isabel. "It was the story; and tell me again, Janey: what was it the poor man said?"

Janey repeated the story. Isabel heard it through with attention, but made no remark. She only sighed deeply, and more than once, as she followed her friend down the cliff.

"We will go to Faith's cottage first!" said Janey. "I am

glad you have something good for her. Some of the neighbors do not like her, because she sets up for a saint, they say; but I never could see any harm in her. As for being better than our neighbors, I suppose we ought all to try to do as well as we can, without thinking of our neighbors."

The posset and marmalet were delivered, and the basket refilled by Faith's oldest girl with periwinkles for Dame Winne; the new baby was duly nursed and admired, and then the friends turned toward Jan Lee's cottage, where Jan himself sat before the door, with his elbows on his knees, smoking his pipe, in calm defiance of King James's counterblast against tobacco. He was a huge, sleepy-looking fisherman, with eyes black and soft as Janey's own, and a flash of wonderfully white teeth amidst his curly black beard.

"This is father, Isabel!" said Janey. "You won't be afraid of him, will you? Daddy, this is Isabel Gray, old Master Jasper's little maid, who was so good to the twins at the feast."

"Eh! And so thou hast brought her to see us," said Jan. "That is right. Come here, my maid. Thou art not afraid of thy friend Janey's father, sure!"

"No!" replied Isabel, promptly putting her little hand into the fisherman's great brown paw. "I am not afraid of you Master Lee. I like you!"

"Why, that's my brave maid!" said the good-natured giant, evidently both amused and pleased. "And why dost thou like me, my lilly? Canst tell?"

"Because I think you are a brave, good man!" replied Isabel. "Because you took Madam Corbet's part when they were going to drown her, and beat that wicked boy who said she was a witch."

"Ay! so you have heard all that tale? Why, my maid, I did only what any brave man would do for my honored master's lady. I had sailed with him, and with his father before him, in the grand old days of Queen Bess. We were but lads both of us when we were with Franky Drake at

"THIS IS FATHER, ISABEL! DADDY, THIS IS ISABEL GRAY."

the taking of St. Jago, and many a hard day we had afterwards together in those latitudes. Harry Corbet saved my life once, when I fell overboard and the shark came after me; and was I going to let his lady be abused and insulted by a parcel of huge shore clodhoppers? Not if she had been the rankest witch that ever flew over to Lundy on a broomstick, instead of being a saint on earth, as she is!"

Jan had grown excited by this time, and Janey, knowing Isabel's timidity, expected to see her slink away. Instead of that, she drew closer to his side, and looked into his face with admiring reverence. Presently, gathering courage, she began to ask him questions about his adventures, and Jan was in the full tide of story-telling when his wife called them in to supper.

The meal was a very pleasant one. The cottage was but a rough place, to be sure, thatched and stone floored, and the rafters were black with the smoke of many generations of driftwood fires; but every thing was neat and clean; there was glass in the casement window, through which the low sun shone brightly, lighting up the strange foreign shells and other curiosities which adorned the walls. There were odd and gaily-painted bits of crockery on the board among the wooden bowls and trenchers, and the prettiest of all, a basin gaily painted with wonderful birds and flowers, was assigned to Isabel. Jan, delighted with a new listener, grew more and more animated, and told marvelous tales of jaguars and howling monkeys, of parrots and humming-birds, of Englishmen freed from Spanish galleys, and of the dispersion of the great Armada; and Isabel listened and marveled and admired to his heart's content.

"Ay, those were brave times," said Jan, at last. "There was something worth living for then. We fought the Spaniards instead of courting them, and getting scrubbed for our pains, and conquered our enemies in fair fight abroad, instead of drowning and burning helpless women at home."

"I wish I had lived then!" said Isabel. "I wish I had

lived under the queen instead of under this Scotchman!"

"I don't believe you love King James very much, Isabel!" said Janey.

"I don't!" returned Isabel, almost fiercely; "I hate him!"

"Hush! hush! That is not safe talk, nor proper talk, for a maid like thee; besides that, a Christian woman should not hate any one!" said Dame Lee, reprovingly. "But you need not look so frightened, dear child!" she added, kindly, as Isabel seemed to shrink into herself at the words. "There was no great harm done, and no one here will repeat thy words."

Isabel's gayety, however, seemed gone for the evening, and she hardly said another word till it was time for her to go home.

"I will go up the cliff with the children, and bring our Janey safe home again!" said Jan, rousing himself.

"Ay, do so; and bring me some honey, for ours is all gone!" said his wife; "and, daddy, you might as well take some fresh shrimps to mistress. They say she is fond of them!"

"So I will! Come, maids, get your hoods!"

"Please, Dame, I did not mean to displease you!" whispered Isabel, as Dame Lee drew her tippet closer about her throat.

"Dear heart! hast thou been fretting over that all this time?" said Dame Lee. "I am not displeased, my lamb; I only meant to give thee a caution; but, Isabel, my dear one, don't let hatred dwell in thy heart towards any one. The king may not be over wise, but he is our king, after all, and sure he has never harmed thee!"

"He *has* harmed me; he has robbed me of every thing— every thing in life!" said Isabel. "I don't want to hate him; but I can't help it, Dame!"

Jane Lee was but a fisherman's wife and daughter; but she had a degree of tact and sense which many a fine lady might have envied. She perceived that the child was growing excited, and though her curiosity was greatly aroused by her words, she refrained from asking any questions.

"Well, well, dear maid, we will say no more; only if I were you, I would pray God for help to forgive my enemy, whoever he was. Think of the dear Lord on the cross praying for his enemies, and it will not seem so hard. Now give me a kiss for good-night, and come to see us again when your aunt can spare you! I wonder what the child has on her mind!" she said to herself, as she stood at her door looking after her husband and the girls. "She is an orphan, I know, and maybe her father has been concerned in some of the troubles of the time. Anyhow, there is a look in her eyes I should be sorry to see in those of any child of mine. I don't believe she is long for this world."

CHAPTER V

THE PERSECUTION

WHEN Isabel went to school the next morning, she saw Peggy Hollins and two or three of the most ignorant of the girls whispering together, and noticed that they stared curiously at her as she passed. These starings and whisperings grew more frequent for the next few days, and presently Isabel saw or imagined that the girls avoided her. The more dull and stupid of them—those with whom Mabel had no patience whatever—had been used to come to her with their books or their work,—more, perhaps, than was quite convenient; but one afternoon, when she offered to help Peggy with her lace, which was always in wonderful disorder, her assistance was rudely refused.

"I want none of your help! I would rather not know any thing than learn as you do!"

"What do you mean?" asked Isabel.

"I knows what I means!" said Peggy, nodding her head. "You are not going to put your spells on me, Mistress Isabel."

Isabel wondered what had come over her; but she thought little of the matter. Peggy had hardly common sense, and she was always getting some odd notion in her head. But as the days went on, and she received the same treatment from several of the other girls,—when even Cicely—who had always been kind to her, in her rough fashion—began to keep out of her away, and to avoid walking home with her, Isabel began to be seriously unhappy, to shrink into herself more than ever, and to start if any one spoke to her.

The sweet-brier pattern was submitted, not to Mrs. Brewster, but to Lady Stantoun, who took great interest in the school, and came in every now and then to see how the lace-making progressed. Lady Stantoun was charmed.

"Why, Isabel, this is beautiful! Did you do this all by yourself?"

"Yes, my lady."

"Did any one ever teach you to draw?"

"No, my lady," replied Isabel, who seemed more distressed than pleased by the lady's praises. "A gentleman gave me a pencil once at the fair, and I used to try to make things with it. And after I saw the lace and embroidering patterns Mistress Brewster showed, I thought that perhaps I might make one for myself."

"And so you have, my child. This would be beautiful worked on satin, with colored silks. I will give you a bit, and some silk, and Mistress Ellenwood or Brewster will show you the stitch. Would you like to try?"

"Oh yes, my lady!" replied Isabel, with the blush and smile which lighted up her pale face so beautifully. "It will be like making something real!" she added.

"You are a strange child!" said Lady Stantoun. "I could find it in my heart to covet you for my own. What say you? Will you come and live with me at the court, and be my little playmate and companion."

"Please, my lady, I could not leave Aunt Bell and Uncle Jasper!" replied Isabel. "They took me when I had no home and no friends. They love me and are kind to me, and I can help Aunt Bell. It would not be right to leave her!"

The girls looked at each other in terror at Isabel's boldness; but the lady only smiled.

"You say truly, Isabel! It would not be right. But you shall have the silks for your work, and a housewife to keep them in, if you will come up to the court this afternoon. Go to the housekeeper's room, and ask for Mrs. Brewster. Now, Mabel, let me see your work. Well, that is better than the last; but you must take more pains before your lace will be fit to wear. Why, how does it happen, Mabel, that you, who used to be queen of the school in every thing, should be so dull about this particular matter of lace-making? I cannot understand it."

"Nor I!" said Mabel, sullenly. "I believe I am bewitched!" She glanced at Isabel as she spoke, and had the malicious pleasure of seeing the expected start, as if some one had hurt her, while three or four of the girls exchanged significant glances.

"Oh, fie! That is an idle excuse!" said Lady Stantoun. "You have learned the knot, as far as I can see, and all you need is care and pains. I fear your mind is busy with something else besides your work. Only draw your threads evenly and closely, and make the knots firm, and your work will be as nice as Isabel's!"

Nothing could be kinder than the lady's tone and manner; but Mabel felt injured, and more than ever angry at Isabel. What business had she to be drawing patterns and to be praised by my lady? Why should she learn embroidery like a born lady? It was too bad! A longing desire for vengeance—a burning wish to inflict some pain or injury upon Isabel—came over her. She might have driven it away by a brave effort, and have been none the worse for it, but even the better; but she did not. She admitted it into her heart, and cherished and petted it, till the evil spirit had full possession. It made no difference that Isabel had never injured her—that, on the contrary, she had tried to help her. Isabel had excelled her. Isabel was liked by every one! Isabel had supplanted her in the affection of the mistress;—so Mabel chose to imagine, though she had no ground for thinking so. And now Isabel had been praised and petted by Lady Stantoun, while she had been blamed and lectured before the whole school. She had a new ground for offence in the discovery, which she had made the night before, that Isabel, instead of being dependent upon her uncle's bounty, as she supposed, had a nice little sum of money of her own, which was safely deposited in the hands of old Master Sarl, the great wool and tobacco merchant of Biddeford. So, with all her other advantages, Isabel was an heiress. These thoughts did not tend to make Mabel more capable of attending to her work or more patient under difficulties. She entangled her bobbins and broke her thread, and, finally, losing all control of herself, she burst into tears. Kind-hearted Lady Stantoun was moved by her distress, and did her best to comfort her, telling her that she would be sure to learn by-and-by, that she must not be discouraged, and finally undid all the good she had done by saying that she was sure Isabel would help her cousin. Mabel dared not give my lady a saucy answer; but she dried her tears and took her work again, and when, after school, Isabel timidly offered her help, she coolly declined her assistance.

"You will have enough to do with your own work, now that you are to learn embroidery: and my lady's favorite should not demean herself by helping common folks."

"Oh, Mabel!" was all Isabel could say.

"Yes; it is easy to say, 'Oh, Mabel!' and look pitiful, now you have done the mischief. If I had the same kind of help as you, maybe I could do as well!"

"I would not have it!" said Peggy Hollins: "no, not for as much gold and jewels as this house would hold. Everyone knows what that kind of thing comes to at last."

"What do you mean by such nonsense as that, Peggy?" asked Janey Lee, cheerfully, as she came up in time to overhear these last remarks.

"Never you mind, Janey Lee! You're like your father: you fear neither God nor devil! Never you mind. Wait and see: that is all!"

"My father fears God, and therefore he doesn't fear the devil!" said Janey. "I don't wonder at any folly or nonsense from Peggy; but I must say, Mabel, I should not have expected to find you listening to her!"

"What have I done?" asked Mabel. "Nothing that I

know of, only that it seems the fashion for every one to find fault with me nowadays."

"You know best what you have done, and what you are doing!" replied Janey, with a penetrating look. "Come, Isabel, never mind them. You are not to go to my lady's this afternoon, are you?"

"No;" she said, on second thought, "I had better not come till Saturday, because she should be busy this afternoon, and out hawking with my lord tomorrow!"

"Well, then, come down to our house! My father bid me tell you he could take us out in the boat when he went to set his lobster pots. You were never in a boat, were you?"

"Take care she does not sink you!" called out Peggy Hollins, after them. "And tell your father to look well to it that the lobsters he catches are not poison. That is the way she casts her spells upon people," she added, turning to Cicely. "Who ever heard of Jan Lee taking such a fancy to any one before?"

Cicely did not like to commit herself, so she replied with a vague shake of the head, which might mean any thing or nothing, and went on her way, wondering, in her foolish head, "whether Isabel really did know more than she had a right to."

From this hour Mabel threw off all disguise. She hated Isabel, and she determined to make her feel it. There was no use, it appeared, in her trying to be a good girl: every one was against her, especially Isabel who had come, as it seemed to her, expressly to be a stumbling-block in her way. It was all Isabel's fault, and Isabel should suffer for it.

Henceforth the poor child's life was miserable indeed. Mabel had found out the sore place in her heart, and she galled it perpetually. She never met Mabel without hearing some allusion to the hated subject—some tale of a witch who had been, or ought to have been, hanged. Every thing was bewitched, according to Mabel. Did one of the girls get a knot in her thread, a stitch run down, a thorn in her hand, she was told to go to Isabel, with an insinuation that she had caused the trouble, and could no doubt cure it, if she were so disposed. The little ones began to shrink from her, or to be withdrawn by their elder sisters, when Isabel tried to pet or assist them; even little Patience Penbuthy looked shyly at her, and refused her proffered cake or sweetmeat. Many of the girls cast significant glances and whispered together when she appeared, and looked scornfully at each other when Mistress Brewster praised her work, as much as to say, "We know where her skill comes from, and we do not envy her."

But if Isabel was rendered miserable, there was one who was more miserable still, and that was Mabel, the author of the mischief. She was smarting under a bitter and mortifying sense of defeat, most galling to her proud and self-confident disposition. She had determined that she would be good;—she would be like the mistress, and be loved and revered, as she was, by everyone. She had had many dreams of the excellence to which she would attain, the poor people she would help, the children she would teach, the sick persons she would nurse, the dying ones she would comfort. She would be known in all the country round as a kind of saint, as her mother's aunt had been, whom she could just remember. She had even begun some of these good works, and had felt very virtuous at the length of her prayers and the chapters she had read out of school in her father's great Bible. More than this, she had begun to have some sense of the beauty and excellence of holiness,—to desire it for its own sake as well as that she might have praise of men. Her conscience had been aroused and enlightened, so that she could, no longer do wrong with impunity. Mabel had had the most comfortable expectations as to her future progress, and already considered herself a very good girl. But she could think so no longer. How could she believe herself a good girl, or likely to become so, while her heart was the nest of every evil passion,—"envy, hatred, malice and all uncharitableness?" Was this the road to the saintship

she coveted: this slandering and persecuting of the innocent?—for innocent Mabel in her heart believed Isabel to
be. She knew that she was serving the devil. And was that
service the way to heaven? Mabel knew better! She knew
that she hated Isabel; that "whosoever hateth his brother
is a murderer," and that "no murderer hath eternal life
abiding in him." She was willing to be a saint so long as
saintship implied no greater sacrifice than that of bodily
ease and comfort. Nay, she really enjoyed such sacrifices.
As a wise and witty author says, "There is nothing easier
and pleasanter than giving up your own will in your own
way." But when it came to giving up her will in the way of
another,—when it came to bearing blame, and deserved
blame, with patience,—to submitting to be excelled in the
place where she had always been first,—to forgiving and
loving one who had, however unconsciously, crossed her
path and humbled her pride, then it was that Mabel for
the first time felt her own helplessness,—then it was that
she saw the evil of her own heart, and knew herself to be
what she always confessed herself in words—a miserable
sinner. There was no such thing as serving two masters.
Mabel knew that well enough. Must she acknowledge
herself in the wrong; humble herself to the mistress and
the girls, and, above all, to Isabel; confess that she had
been guilty of a malicious slander; own that Isabel was
the best scholar and the best workwoman, and submit to
take the place in the estimation of her companions which
belonged to her? She could not do it! Must she, then, give
up all her dreams of being a saint and of going to heaven?
It seemed so.

And suppose she succeeded ever so well in what she
had undertaken? Suppose she drove Isabel from the
school, made her miserable, even caused her death, by
the bad name she brought upon her, as was likely enough
in that time and place. What good would that do her?
The fact would still remain the same that Isabel was the
best scholar and the best workwoman. If Isabel was dead,

indeed,—Mabel turned in horror from that thought at
first; but it came again and again, and at last she began
to entertain it.

Saturday came, and Isabel made her visit at the great
house, as she been desired.

"Go by all means!" said Dame Winne, when Isabel
asked her permission; "but don't you go building too much
upon what my lady said. Like as not she never gave it
another thought. That is often the way with great ladies
when they promise favors to poor folks. Not as I am saying any thing against this present lady; but I know how
my old lady, my lord's mother, served me about the fowls
she promised me." And then came the oft-told story about
the Spanish fowls which my lady had promised to Dame
Winne, and then given away to Gammer Styles at the
Millheads,—a wrong which the good woman had never
forgotten or quite forgiven.

Nevertheless Isabel could not help expecting a good
deal from her visit; nor was she disappointed. The housekeeper received her graciously, and entertained her with
saffron-cake and a glass of mead. Mistress Brewster led
her through the house, and showed her all the fine furniture and pictures, and finally took her to my lady's
withdrawing-room, where Lady Stantoun received her
with her usual kindness, showed her her own ivory and
ebony embroidery-frame, with its flowers,—which looked,
Isabel declared, as though one might smell them,—and
even allowed her to do a dozen stitches in one corner.
Prim Mrs. Brewster, looking on with some private doubts
as to her lady's discretion in taking so much notice of the
little school-girl, observed with satisfaction that Isabel's
head did not seem in the least turned by all this attention.
Isabel replied in her low, sweet voice, without pertness or
forwardness, to the questions asked her, and volunteered
no remarks of her own, and it was impossible to be offended at the look of innocent exultation which came over
the girl's face when she found that she had really worked

a leaf. Lady Stantoun was very much pleased with her little visitor, and at parting she opened her work-table drawer and gave Isabel not only the promised materials for her work, but a pretty housewife, or thread case, made of brocade, and having its stitched apartments filled with skeins of silk and thread. Nor was this all: she produced a good-sized bundle of bits of silk and cloth of different sorts.

"Would you like these pieces?" she said. "I dare say you are above dressing babies; but most girls can find use for such things!"

Isabel could hardly believe in her good fortune. Visions of cushions and housewives for the mistress and her other friends, of a purse for Master Lee, and a doll for the twins, flitted across her imagination.

"Oh, my lady! are all these for me, and to do what I please with?"

"Surely, sweet heart, what else!" said the lady, pleased to see the pleasure she had given so easily. "And, Isabel, I wish you to carry these books to the mistress as you go home. When you have finished your embroidery you may bring it to show to me or Mrs. Brewster!"

Isabel curtseyed and went on her way home. As she came near the end of the avenue, she met Meg Hollins, Peggy's sister, who was dairy-maid at the Court, carrying her full pail on her head. Meg had heard from her sister of the notice which Lady Stantoun had taken of Isabel, and was prepared to resent it as an injury to herself.

"Oh, ho! my fine lady!" she cried out, in her coarse voice. "So you have been up to the Court to see my lady, forsooth! while honest folks, whose families have lived on the lands for years, cannot get so much as a look. But take care, my fine dame! Pride must have a fall!"

Meg was destined to illustrate her own maxim sooner than she expected, for as, forgetting her pail, she tossed her head in virtuous contempt of Isabel's supposed presumption, her foot slipped, and she came very near depositing herself and her burden in the ditch by the roadside. As it was, she was pretty well splashed by the milk she carried.

"So that is the way you serve me, is it!" she cried out, as soon as she had recovered herself. "Well, well! never you mind. Maybe our time will come, and then it is not my lady's favor that will save you, my fine mistress."

Isabel saw that there was no use trying to justify herself, and she hurried away, feeling that her pleasure for the day was gone. She found the mistress sitting under the arbor in her little garden, and delivered the books and the lady's message.

"And did my lady give you the silks for your embroidery? Let me see them, my dear! But, Isabel, what is the matter?" she exclaimed, as she saw how pale the child was and how her hands trembled. "Has any thing frightened you, my maid?"

"No, please mistress, but——"

The sobs would come in spite of her. She burst into tears, and not all her respect for the mistress could prevent the distress which had been accumulating so long from having its way. The pent-up waters had burst their bounds, and they must needs run till they were exhausted.

"Oh, my heart will break! my heart will break!" she sobbed. "Oh, if I had but died with my mother! What shall I do? Oh, if I had never been born!"

"Hush! hush! my dear maid," said Elizabeth, taking the child in her arms. "Do not say such things. Whatever be your grief for your mother, God can comfort you, and he surely will, if you but call upon him!"

Isabel almost shrieked, "No, no! he will not! Oh, if he would! If he would but have heard my prayer! My mother loved him, and served him all her life, and he failed her at last. He left her to the malice of her enemies!"

"What do you mean, Isabel?" asked Elizabeth, seeing plainly that Isabel had something more than any of the ordinary troubles of childhood to distress her. "What was the matter with your mother?"

Isabel's eyes dilated, and her features seemed to stiffen with horror.

"Don't you know?" she gasped. "They said she was a witch?"

Elizabeth comprehended the horror at once. She knew all that was implied in those words. Isabel threw herself on her knees, with her face buried in her lap, and in brief and interrupted sentences told all the dreadful tale. Her mother had been a dairy-woman, owning her own little farm in the neighborhood of Malvern, and carrying eggs, cream, and butter to the people who came to the Springs. She was uniformly lucky with her dairy products; her butter would come in the hottest weather, and was always yellow and hard. Her hens laid the year round, and her cream-cheese and cheese-cakes never hung heavy on her hands. Withal she was a godly Christian woman, and had the reputation of being a Puritan,—that is, she read her Bible a great deal, always went to church, and utterly refused to have any thing whatever to do with the Sunday games authorized by King James's famous Book of Sports, openly declaring that such a use of the holy day was heathenish and shameful, and a disgrace to a Christian land. Perhaps she was less charitable than she might have been to the failings of her neighbors; perhaps her increasing popularity as a dairywoman, and consequent prosperity, moved them to envy; but certain it is that the engine so terribly ready in those days, in the hands of ignorance and malice, was brought to bear, and an accusation of witchcraft was laid upon Isabel Gray. There is no need to repeat all the horrid details which Isabel whispered to Elizabeth Ellenwood. It is enough to say that, after undergoing unspeakable abuse at the hands of the ignorant mob, and the no less ignorant parish officers, she was condemned and put to death, as hundreds of men and women had been before her, under the reign of the Scottish Solomon who had succeeded to the English throne. Little Isabel was with difficulty preserved from the hands of her

mother's executioners by the exertions of the parish clergyman,—who had tried in vain to save Dame Gray,—after
receiving injuries which she would feel all her life long.

"My mother was a good woman," said Isabel. "She
loved God, and prayed to him always; and yet he left her
to the malice of her enemies. He would not hear her nor
me, though she had served him all her life."

Elizabeth saw it all. Here was this poor child bearing a
burden under which the strongest man might have sunk,
and all the time thinking herself forgotten and deserted
by that heavenly Father whom she had been taught to
love and trust above all. No wonder she was sad and reserved! No wonder that her cheek was blanched, her eyes
downcast, and her step heavy!

Elizabeth hardly knew how to deal with the case before her; but she raised her heart to him whose name is
"The Comforter," and begged for his aid who had promised strength according to the day.

"Isabel!" said she, softly, at last, "you think that God
did not love your mother because he suffered her to be
evil-entreated and finally to be overcome by her enemies.
You think he deserted your mother in the needful time of
trouble, because he did not interfere to save her life. But
now tell me, did he not love his only-begotten Son? Yet
he suffered him to be for a time overcome by the malice
of his enemies. He permitted that Son to pray, and, as it
seemed, in vain, 'Father, if it be possible, let this cup pass
from me!'"

Isabel raised her colorless face, and gazed at her friend
as though she would read her very soul.

"But that was to save the world?" she said, after a
pause. "My mother's death did no one any good!"

"That is more than you can say, my child. You tell me
that your mother died like a true saint, praying for her
murderers to the last. Who can say what precious seed
may have been sown by her example! Right dear in the
sight of the Lord is the death of his saints!"

"But he raised his Son from the dead!"

"True, and wherefore? For this reason, among others, that the grave and gate of death might have no more terrors for his children. I doubt not that your dear mother went at once from the stake to the glories of paradise,— from the shouts of the rabble and their cruel mockings to the songs of angels and the sight of her Savior's face. Isabel, my dear one, when we are once at his feet, it will matter little to us how we got there. Oh, my maid, never, never doubt his love or his faithfulness. He has not promised that we shall not pass through the waters, but that when we do pass through them, he will be with us. 'In the world ye shall have tribulation!' were the words of the greatest of all sufferers to his followers; but he hastened to add, 'Be of good cheer! I have overcome the world.' If I understand aright, a part of the malice of the crowd against your mother arose from her steadfastly upholding the honor of God's law and his day. She was 'persecuted for righteousness' sake,' and 'blessed' are they who are so persecuted, 'for theirs is the kingdom of heaven.'"

Isabel drew a long, deep breath. "If it were only true," she said. "If I could only dare to think so!"

"My child, dare to trust God for all. Your needs can never go beyond his love. 'He that spared not his own Son, but delivered him up freely for us all, how shall he not with him freely give us all things.' Isabel, think of it!—his own Son!"

Isabel remained kneeling by her friend, but she no longer wept or hid her face. Her eyes seemed fixed on something far away beyond the horizon of sea and sky, seen through the open lattice, and her face wore a rapt expression, as if her thoughts were in another world.

"I see it all!" she murmured, at last. "I seem to see it all! Oh, if he is true, let every man be a liar! I can bear it all!"

"Thank God that you see the light at last!" said the mistress, fervently. "And, Isabel, if the cloud comes back, as perhaps it may, do not look at it. Remember the clouds pass, but the sun shines the same, even though we cannot see it; and wait patiently for his time. Remember, too, that the 'clouds drop down the dew,' and that the gloomy, rainy days send the 'springs into the valleys which run among the hills.'"

As Elizabeth went through the garden with Isabel, she was surprised by meeting Mabel, who was standing among the shrubs under the window, with a basket on her arm, Mabel started like a guilty thing.

"What are you doing here?" asked the mistress, a little coldly, for Mabel's position and appearance were certainly suspicious.

"I came to bring you this basket from my mother," replied Mabel, "and I thought you had company with you, so I did not go in. If I had known it was Isabel, I would not have waited outside."

It might be all so, and Elizabeth was not given to suspicion. She welcomed Mabel kindly, and detained her some time to show her the new books which Lady Stantoun had lent her; but after Mabel had gone, she could not help saying to herself, "If it were any one but Mabel, I should think she had been listening under the window."

"So that is the story of Isabel's dislike to the king and her faintishness about witches!" thought Mabel, as she walked slowly homeward. "So her own mother was killed for a witch! No wonder she does not like to hear about it. A respectable ancestry, truly! Well, it is natural she should be sore about it, and perhaps she has not meant any harm after all. I will tease her no more."

CHAPTER VI

THE HOUSEWIFE

ON Sunday morning it was customary for the girls of
Lady Rosamond's school to assemble at their school-
house, and walk to church in procession, two and two, the
mistress and the head girl bringing up the rear, and the
two next older girls marshalling the head of the column and
taking care of the "babes." The office heretofore devolved
upon Janey Lee and her cousin Emma, a good steady, dull
girl, whom everybody liked and laughed at. But Emma had
gone to service in a farmer's family during the last week,
and, to the joy of both friends, it fell to the lot of Isabel to
take her place. Before they set out, the mistress announced
to her flock that she should be obliged to go to Exeter for a
few days, to attend to business of her own, and that Lady
Stantoun had kindly granted to the girls a week's holiday.
The school then fell into its usual order, and the little train
took its way over the green toward the church.

"How glad I am you will always walk with me, Isabel!"
said Janey, who, being of a lively disposition, had, truth
to tell, sometimes been oppressed by her cousin's dull
goodness. "We shall sit together in church, and in school
too, for of course you will take Emma's place. Are you not
glad?"

"Yes; *indeed* I am!" replied Isabel. "Oh, Janey, you don't
know how glad!"

Something in the tone made Janey look at her friend.
"What was the change which had come over Isabel, bringing light to her eye, a spring to her languid step, and even
a fresh blush of color to her marble cheek?"

"Why, Isabel, what has happened to you?" asked Janey. "You look ten years younger than you did yesterday!"

"I *feel* so!" said Isabel, with emphasis. "But, Janey, we must not talk, or we shall have the babes all chattering at once!" As they came together at the church door, she whispered to her friend, "Janey, it was all the mistress! She made me see the goodness of God!"

The school children were accustomed to sing in church; but heretofore Isabel's voice had never been heard among them. Now, however, at the chant,

> "Oh, come let us sing unto the Lord!"

it arose with a fullness and sweetness which made more than one person look round to see who was the new singer. The girls looked at each other in amazement, and Elizabeth—the only one who understood the matter—thanked God in her heart that she had been allowed to be the instrument of leading this little one of his heartily to rejoice in the strength of his salvation.

"Did you ever hear the like of Isabel's singing?" said Cicely, after church, to Mabel. "It was just so in the prayers. She seemed to pray with her very soul, as if her whole heart went up with the words. Well, say what you will, I do not believe there is any harm in that girl. I don't believe any one who was serving evil spirits could sing and pray in that way!"

"As to that!" said Mabel, "parson said only this morning that Satan could transform himself into an angel of light! However, I don't mean to say that Isabel does have any thing to do with evil spirits!" she added, remembering her resolution not to speak unkindly of Isabel. "That would be going too far!"

"You *have* said so, any way, Mabel Winne!" said Cicely, "You told me yourself that you would not have such help as Isabel had for any thing. You have said such things ever so many times, and all the girls have heard you!"

"You might have known that I only spoke so to tease Isabel!" said Mabel, vexed to find her own words remembered and quoted against her.

"Then you ought to be ashamed of yourself!" returned Cicely, warmly. "You used to say you would never tell a lie, even in joke. You have set all the girls, except the Lees, against that poor maid, and now you turn round and say you did not mean any thing. It is a shame!"

Mabel drew herself up and walked away in a very stately manner, without answering Cicely's last words; but she felt any thing but elevated in her own eyes. It was true she had, to gratify her own spite and envy, brought up an evil report upon her innocent cousin, and now she was to find out—what all evildoers find out sooner or later—how much more easily mischief is done than undone.

"Mabel!" said her mother to her, the next morning, "how wilt thou like to spend thy week's holiday with grandmother, at Langham?"

Mabel's eyes sparkled.

"Father is going over with barley to the maltster to-day, and you can ride behind him. Grandmother will be glad of your help and your company, and it will be a nice change for you!"

Mabel was very glad to go. She was a great favorite with her grandmother, who always petted her, and praised her as the cleverest maid in Devonshire. She thought, too, that she should like to be out of the way of the school-girls, and, above all, out of the way of Isabel. She took care to be ready exactly at the appointed time, so as not to put her father out of humor by making him wait for her; and after a prosperous journey of twelve miles, she was safely deposited in her grandmother's kitchen, at Langham.

More people than Cicely wondered at the change which had come over Isabel; but nobody rejoiced over it more than good Dame Winne. It had been a grief to her that Isabel should be so sad—so unlike a child.

"Not that there is any fault to find with her!" she had said to her husband. "No creature could be more handy about the house: and the mistress says she is the same in school; but it seems so unnatural for a girl of her age never to sing or laugh about her work, and hardly ever to speak of her own accord. Then she is so timid! If any stranger comes into the house, she shrinks away out of the room, or if she cannot, she seems scared at being spoken to. She has not made friends with any one except big Jan Lee, and 'tis odd how she takes to him!"

"Think of all she has been through!" replied old Jasper. "Think of her seeing her poor mother killed before her eyes, and herself almost murdered at the same time. 'Tis no wonder that she cannot abide the name of King James. Well-a-day! 'Twas an evil day when the Scotchman came to rule over the Englishmen. Far better would it have been, to my thinking, had our good queen married like another woman, and had a son to succeed her."

But now all seemed changed with Isabel. She was heard singing in the morning over her work, in the garden as she weeded the borders, in the meadow where she gathered the cowslips for wine. Her step was light and quick, and her face lighted up with a smile whenever any one spoke to her. She kept herself as busy as a bee, till Dame Winne declared that she worked harder in holiday time than in school time. Her embroidery succeeded marvelously, and she was very much engaged in making a housewife, as exactly as possible like the one Lady Stantoun had given her.

"Aunt Bell, may I go down and see Janey Lee this afternoon, and ask how Faith is going on?" asked Isabel.

"Surely, my dear maid," replied her aunt. "You may take a basket with some strawberries to Faith and also a little pot of the butter I churned this morning. The poor woman does not get on well, and though folks call her a Puritan, I can see no harm in her, unless that she talks more like parson than is fitting for common folks to do!"

"I know she never says any thing wrong!" said Isabel. "I cannot remember that I ever heard her speak an unkind word of anybody. I like Faith. She makes me think of my mother!"

It was the first time Isabel had ever mentioned her mother since she came to Stantoun-Corbet.

"Then she makes thee think of a saint of the Lord!" replied the old Dame: "as thy dear mother was, by all accounts, if ever one lived in the world. Well, go thy way, dear, and I will get the basket ready!"

Isabel had no longer any fear of going down the cliff. On the contrary, she enjoyed it; but she had to walk the length of the village street first, and in doing so she was pretty sure of meeting with something disagreeable. Mabel's mischief had gone farther than she dreamed of. Peggy Hollins had told at home all that she had heard about Isabel at school. She had two or three brothers, rude, ignorant, lads, the dread of every cat, dog, and cow in the village, and always ripe for any mischief. They were among those who had felt the weight of the wrath of Jan Lee and his sons at the time of Madam Corbet's persecution; but that did not keep them from being ready for another performance of the same kind. They had more than once shouted after Isabel as she crossed the green, and she stood in mortal terror of them. Two or three of the girls also turned out of the way to avoid meeting her, and whispered together significantly as she passed by. Isabel hurried along the street, nor slackened her pace till she reached the top of the cliff. Then she paused to rest a little, and began leisurely to descend the steep path, stopping now and then to look around her or to gather some little wild flowers. She had got about half way down when she heard a cry of distress, which seemed to come from the face of the cliff. At first she thought it was one of the many birds which build in the crevices and on the ledges of the rocks. She stopped and listened. The cry was repeated, and was too plainly that of a hurt or frightened child. Isabel looked along the face of the cliff, and for a moment her heart almost stood still, for there, in the most dangerous place, close to the waterfall and directly over Dobby's pool, she saw a small figure in a green frock and red tippet, which could be no other than little Patience. A sort of blind path led away from the trodden track at this point, following the ledge of rocks till it ended, to all appearance, at a projecting stone, beyond which there was clearly no passing. Close to this stone, in the very spray of the fall, crouched the child, clinging desperately to the rugged root of a birch which grew above her head, and crying for help.

Isabel hesitated for a moment. What should she do? Should she run back to the village, or down to the Cove and call for help? If she did the first, she feared to meet only the Hollins boys, for the other lads were either in school or wheat-hoeing with their fathers. If she ran down to the Cove, it was more likely than not that all the men were out fishing? There was clearly no time to lose. Patience was already very wet with the spray, and the breeze was blowing fresh and cool. She might become chilled through and lose her hold, or she might try to return alone over the dangerous path.

With an intensity of faith, Isabel lifted her heart to her heavenly Father for help, and then, setting down her basket, she began carefully to make her way along the narrow shelving and slippery ledge of rocks.

"I am coming, Patience, my dear!" she called to the child. "Isabel is coming to take you home. Keep quite still and do not look down!"

Jan Lee and his two sons were below on the beach, leisurely preparing their boat to slip out to sea with the afternoon tide, when Faith Dean, who had ventured outside her door for the first time since her illness, came running along the beach with her infant in her arms like one distracted.

"Why, what ails the woman?" cried Jan. "Will you kill yourself and the babe to boot?"

"Look up at the cliff, Jan Lee!" repeated poor Faith. "Look up and see those little maids, and save them, if you be a man!"

Jan cast one look in the direction indicated. It was enough. He saw it all.

"Bring that new rope and the axe!" he said, with a calm voice, as the people who were at their doors and windows came running together. "Some of you take this poor creature into the house. You that be men, follow me!"

The alarm had now been given from above that a child had got astray on the cliff, and a crowd was collected on the edge and on the path; but no one had ventured on the ledge, along which Isabel was carefully making her way, turning her face from the sea, and holding on by roots and briars till she reached the child.

"Now, then, Patience, hold fast with one hand, and reach the other to me!" she said, in a clear, cheerful voice, which was distinctly heard above the dashing water. "Be brave and steady, and we shall soon be safe. Never mind the bird,—as a gull came sweeping over and hovered round their heads with angry screams,—he will not hurt us. Now, take firm short steps, and keep hold of my hand!"

With great docility the trembling little one did as she was directed, though it seemed as though her chilled limbs could hardly support her. Carefully and slowly they returned over the slippery shelving path, which seemed in some places to crumble under their feet. It appeared to those who looked on in breathless silence as though every step would be the last. There was no helping them either, for no man could venture to trust his weight upon the ledge.

"I shall fall, Isabel, and drag you down too!" said the little one, despairingly. "Let me go, and save yourself!"

"Never!" replied Isabel, firmly. "I will save you or die with you. Courage, now! One more great effort, and you are safe."

Thus encouraged, Patience made another effort. Isabel took one more step, and as she passed her arm forward seeking for the supports that had upheld her before, she felt her hand taken in the firm clasp of "little Jan Lee," as he was called, who stood at the end of a line of men, holding hands around the corner of the cliff; and the two girls were drawn upon the firm ground. The next moment Isabel was in the arms of big Jan, who kissed her and cried over her like a woman over her baby.

"There! what think you of that, you lads above there!" shouted Jan Lee. "How long will it be before one of you will do as much as this poor maid here? But what under heaven took you on that path, Isabel?"

"I went to save Patience!" replied Isabel, simply. "Do some one take the poor babe home and put her to bed! She is drenched through and through. Cicely, do take your cousin home, before she gets her death in this wind."

"And what are *you* getting, I should like to know!" cried Cicely, throwing her arms round Isabel's neck. "Oh, Isabel, how could I ever believe any harm of you?"

"Because you were a fool!" said Jan Lee, roughly, but not unkindly. "As for you Hollinses, let me hear one of you breathe a word against my maid,—ay, you know what I mean,—and, lad or maid, I will put you where you won't get out in a hurry."

So saying, Jan marched up the cliff and across the green, leading Isabel, who could hardly persuade him that she was able to walk.

Mabel returned home on Saturday night. She had been happier at Langham than for a long time before. With no one to oppose or thwart her, with her grandmother and the maids to make much of her, and exalt her in her own eyes, with the parson to praise her reading, and hold her up to his own daughters as an example, she easily recovered her self-complacency, and with it much of her good-humor. It was easy to feel magnanimous and forgiving towards Isabel at that distance, and when she had no rivalry to apprehend from her. She read in her grandmother's Bible, and went to church, and talked to her little cousins about being good children and saying their prayers, and began again to indulge in the old dream of saintship.

In this frame of mind she came home, and was met directly by the story of Isabel's exploit in rescuing little Patience from a dreadful death. Isabel's praises were in every one's mouth, and all the Penbuthy tribe were ready to worship her, Cicely included. Something of the old feeling of bitterness arose in Mabel's heart. She assented to every thing that her mother had to say in praise of Isabel, though she professed to think it no great feat, after all.

"Any one could go along that ledge who was not a coward!" said she; "but then it certainly was a good deal for Isabel to do, who is afraid of her own shadow. I suppose she will be greater than ever with parson and the mistress. But a new broom sweeps clean, we all know."

As soon as the girls were dismissed after church, Mabel was joined by Peggy Hollins, whom she would gladly have avoided; but Peggy would not be put off.

"I suppose you have heard all this about Isabel and Patience!" said she. "They make a great fuss over her! For my part, whatever they may say about Patience having gone after the kitten she was bringing home, and which got away from her, nobody will make me believe that she got where Isabel found her by herself. Them that hides can find! And do you know, Mabel, Isabel went up to the great house last Saturday was a week, and Mistress Brewster took her all over, and showed her every thing; yes, even into my lady's own room, and, more than that, my lady let her work on her own frame:—more by token;—they say she worked better than my lady herself, though she never touched it before."

"Nonsense!" said Mabel. "I dare say she went into the housekeeper's room, and she might be sent for to speak to my lady; though 'tis more likely, to my mind, that Isabel made the story out of whole cloth. A likely thing, to be sure!"

"Isabel never made the story at all, then!" returned Peggy. "She has never said a word about it to any one, unless it might be Janey Lee. My sister Meg told me, and she had it from John Footman, who had just come into the room to take my lady's orders. And he saw Isabel work on the frame, and saw the bud she made; so there, now! And my lady gave her a housewife, and a great bundle of silks and satins, for Meg saw them! So, now, what do you think of that? Is not my lady bewitched, like the rest?"

"It is very strange!" replied Mabel "but I have heard that great ladies are apt to take such fancies. How did Meg come to see what my lady gave Isabel?"

"Meg was coming up the avenue with her milk pail on her head, when she met Isabel coming down, and just as she passed she slipped, and splashed the milk all over her new kettle and apron. The housekeeper scolded her well for it; but Meg says she will take her Bible oath it was Isabel who made her miss her footing."

Mabel bade her companion good night, and turned towards home, with all the old angry and envious feelings rising up stronger than ever. Isabel, the idol of half the village! Isabel, petted by my lady as if she had been her own child, publicly commended by the parson, and more than ever by her old uncle and aunt! Mabel felt herself robbed and defrauded. It was in no amiable mood that she encountered Isabel and Janey in the porch of Lady Rosamond's school next morning. Isabel was exhibiting to Janey a handsome housewife or needle-case, furnished with scissors, thread, and needles all complete. As she saw Mabel she look confused, and seemed as if about to hide the housewife, but still held it in her hand as she returned Mabel's somewhat constrained greeting.

"Isn't Isabel's housewife beautiful?" said Janey, seeing Mabel's eyes fixed upon it.

A little before, Mabel would have given a great deal to possess such a housewife; but she was not going to give Isabel the pleasure of hearing it praised. She answered, contemptuously enough,—

"I don't see any thing pretty about it!—an old, faded-looking thing! I think my lady might have given you something better than that!"

Isabel colored and the tears came into her eyes; but she put the housewife into her pocket and said no more. A while afterwards, as the girls were getting ready for their work, Mabel saw Janey take this very housewife out of her basket and lay it on her desk. It was her business as head girl to report violations of the rules, and there was a short one against borrowing. It was not without a feeling of satisfaction that she said aloud,—

"Mistress, Jane Lee has borrowed Isabel Gray's thread-case, and is using it herself."

Isabel turned scarlet, and Jane looked up, but there was more fun than confusion in her face.

"How is that, Jane?" asked the mistress.

"Please, mistress, it is not Isabel's, but mine!" replied Janey. "She gave it me only this morning!"

"Oh, fie, Isabel!" said the mistress, now really displeased. "Did you give away the thread-case my lady gave you?"

"No, please, mistress!" replied Isabel; and then, as she saw Elizabeth waited for an explanation, she added, "I made it after the pattern of my lady's for a present for Mabel; but she did not like it, and so I gave it to Janey!"

"How did you know she did not like it?" asked the mistress.

"Please, mistress, she said so!" answered Janey, as Isabel hesitated. "She saw Isabel showing it to me, and said it was a shabby old thing. She did not know it was for her, though!" added Janey, with a tone of great simplicity: "she thought it was the one my lady gave to Isabel!"

Every one guessed the true state of the case at once, and a subdued titter passed through the school, nor could Elizabeth herself avoid smiling.

"We will say no more about it!" said she. "The next time Isabel makes a present, I trust she will be more lucky. Meantime I wish you joy of your thread-case, Janey. It is really a beautiful piece of work, and does the maker credit."

There was much in this remark to please Isabel, though she was sorry for Mabel's discomfiture. She was busy at home making a similar case for the mistress, which was destined to throw Jane's entirely into the shade.

"So, Mabel, you missed it that time!" exclaimed one of the girls, as Mabel made her appearance on the playground. "'Many a slip 'twixt cup and lip,' you see. Another time don't be in such a hurry to run down another's goods."

"Ay, and such a slip!" said another. "Why, it is even prettier than my lady's own. Where did you get the stuff, Isabel?"

Mabel had resolved only that morning that no provocation whatever should make her speak an unkind word to Isabel; but she had reckoned without her host. She had expected no such trial as this. Thus to lose at once the very thing she most desired, and to be made the butt of her companions' jokes and laughter in consequence,—it was too much for the will which was fortified only by weak human resolution. The desire to be revenged on Isabel in the readiest way came uppermost, and she answered the last speaker deliberately, and in a voice which could be heard all over the playground,—

"Don't you know, Mary? 'Tis a piece of her mother's best gown,—the one she wore when she was burned for a witch!"

There was a moment's silence, and then Janey Lee sprang to Isabel's side.

"You wicked, wicked girl! you have killed her!" she exclaimed.

"So much the better!" said Mabel, with a hard laugh. "I have saved Gaffer Grinwood the trouble, and there is one witch the less to tangle folk's thread and lead little children astray."

"She has not killed me!" said Isabel, speaking in a clear, steady voice, though she was pale as ashes, and leaned on Janey to support herself. "Mabel, I do not know how you have learned this secret; but it is true. My dear mother—a saint of God if ever there was one—was slain by wicked hands for a witch. You may bring the same fate upon me, for aught I know: you seem trying to do it; but you can do me no real harm. God is my hope and strength, and to him I commit my ways. 'Fear not them which kill the body,' and after that have no more that they can do; but, Mabel, fear him who after death is able to cast both body and soul into hell! May God forgive you, and bring you to a better mind." So saying, she took Janey's arm and walked away, followed by Cicely and the Penbuthy girls, her cousins.

Nobody said a word for some seconds after Isabel withdrew. Then Peggy Hollins spoke.

"Well, Mabel, if any harm happens to you after this, we shall know who to lay it to. How she did curse you, to be sure!"

"I don't see that!" returned Mary. "'Twas more like a blessing than a curse, to my thinking. But tell us, Mabel, was Isabel's mother really a witch!"

"She was burned for one!" replied Mabel. "I know that for certain."

"Anyhow, that does not make Isabel one!" persisted Mary. "I do believe, Mabel, you told that for mere spitefulness, because you were vexed about the thread-case. It was not like a witch, or any thing else bad, that she went along the ledge after little Patience, the other day."

"Well, now, to my thinking, that looks worse than all the rest!" said another girl. "How did she get over that place, where a goat could not go in safety. As for the child's going after the kitten she lost, that may be so; but what then? Faith Dean, down at the Cove, gave her the creature, and we all know that Faith is a good friend of Isabel."

"To be sure!" said another; and then followed tale after tale, each more foolish than the last, about witches and their doings, till Mabel, alarmed at the storm she had raised, attempted in vain to quiet it by turning the

conversation to the coming trial for Lady Stantoun's prizes. She only increased the tumult. Of what use was it trying for the prizes when there was one among them who
could make my lady think and see just what she pleased?

"After all, I don't care!" said Mabel, as she walked
home-ward. "I don't suppose they will kill her, and if they
only make her leave the town, it will be a good riddance
indeed!"

Mabel had said her prayers very carefully every night
and morning since she left home. But she did not say them
this night, nor many days after.

CHAPTER VII

THE ROOT BEARS FRUIT

How do you suppose Mabel found out about your mother, Isabel?" asked Janey. She had drawn Isabel to a seat under the great elm, and Ellen Penbuthy had run to bring her some fresh water.

"I cannot guess!" replied Isabel. "No one, I think, knows it here except my uncle and aunt and the mistress, unless it is parson. I have sometimes thought he knew, because he always seems so sorry for me!"

"Perhaps your aunt told Mabel's father and mother!" suggested Janey.

"No, I am sure she did not. She told me only yesterday that she had never said a word to any one. She did not quite like it, because I told the mistress, though she believed the mistress would never speak of it again."

"When did you tell the mistress, Isabel?" asked Cicely, abruptly.

"Last Saturday. It was when I came from the great house. My lady sent me with some books to the mistress, and then I told her all about it."

"I thought as much!" said Cicely. "I see the whole matter as plain as a pike-staff."

"What do you mean, Cicely?" asked Ellen Penbuthy.

"Saturday afternoon I was up in our garret!" said Cicely, "and I saw Isabel go into the stone cottage with her parcels. Presently Mabel came in through the garden with a basket. The casement was open, and Mabel stopped and stood under it ever so long, as still as a mouse. Then when she heard mistress opening the door, she came forward as though she had just come in. Depend upon it, she listened and heard all that Isabel said."

"I can't think Mabel would do such a thing as to listen!" said Isabel, "though I knew she was standing close under the window when mistress opened the door."

"What a pity you told mistress!" said Ellen.

"I am not sorry!" said Isabel. "I would not miss the comfort she gave me for any thing. She put new life into me. I am sorry it is known, because people will talk, and it will trouble Uncle Jasper and Aunt Bell; but, girls, I am not ashamed of my mother,—no more ashamed of her than if she was one of the Christian martyrs we read about in mistress's great book sometimes. I don't wish to accuse any falsely; but I believe it was fully as much the people's spite at her for being what they called a Puritan, for her godly life and her speaking against the Sunday games, as because she was believed to be a witch."

"Did she speak against the games?" asked Cicely.

"Yes; she said they were only fit for heathens, and not for a Christian land: that it made no difference what good words parson might preach in the morning, so long as they were driven out of people's heads by dancing and ball-playing and drinking in the afternoon. She never would go near the green, or let me go; and she persuaded some of our neighbors to come to our house and read the Bible with us in the afternoon."

"Parson Parnell does not like the Sunday sports, I know!" said Janey; "but my lord favors them. It does not seem just the way to spend the Lord's day, does it? One cannot think of the apostles sitting round on the ale bench before the 'Rose,' drinking and talking about the girls' dancing."

"Janey, you wicked girl!" cried Ellen, very much shocked; "how dare you say such a thing?"

"If it would be wrong for them, it would be wrong for us, and if it was wrong then, it is wrong now!" persisted Janey. "Do you think it was that which set the people against your mother, Isabel?"

"Partly, but not altogether! My mother was very lucky in all her work. She never had her butter soft or cheesy, or her cream and milk sour, and she could sell more than any one else at the wells. All the fine ladies and gentlemen who came to drink of the waters bought of her, and she made a deal of money. I think it was only because she was so careful to have every thing about her dairy so sweet and clean, and to keep all the beasts and fowls in good case. But there were two old women near us who kept a dairy, and they were vexed because mother did so much better than they; so they got up the story that my mother had a familiar spirit. Our old black cat used to climb up on a tree and jump into the chamber window, and they said that he was an imp. I had several little brothers and sisters who died when they were babies, and these women declared that my mother killed them to feed her black cat, and that my father died in the same way! and some people were silly enough to believe them."

"What wicked wretches!" exclaimed Cicely. "I should think you would hate them."

"I pray that I may forgive them, as my dear mother did before she died!" said Isabel, solemnly. "She sent them a message from the prison, that she forgave them and prayed for them!"

"She was like a saint in the Acts of the Martyrs!" said Cicely, in a tone of awe. "Isabel, can you forgive Mabel?"

"God will help me to forgive her!" replied Isabel, in a low tone. "My mother could not have done it but for his help. I see that now. He was with her in the prison, and all through that dreadful time, and I believe he will be with me;" and she repeated, as if to herself, "When thou passest through the water, I will be with thee, and through the rivers, they shall not overflow thee; for I am the Lord, thy God; the Holy One of Israel, thy Savior."

"Well, I know one thing!" said Cicely, after a little pause; "I will take care that mistress knows where Mabel got her knowledge."

"No, please, don't tell her!" implored Isabel. "It would do no good, only make her more vexed with me. I can't think what I have done to make her hate me so!" she added, sadly.

"You have done something which she could not, and that is enough!" returned Janey. "Mabel has a jealous disposition. I always knew that from the first time she threw away the cake Dame Huson gave her, because she thought Emma's was a little larger."

"I shall not promise not to tell, Isabel!" said Cicely, as Isabel continued to urge her. "I shall use my own judgment; but I will not say a word unless it seems to me to be necessary." And with this Isabel was obliged to be satisfied.

Isabel soon felt the influence of Mabel's communication. The next morning, as she was coming to school, two or three boys called out. "There goes the witch's daughter! I say, mistress, how long since you took a ride on a broomstick!" with other witticisms of a similar nature.

Isabel hurried along; but she could not help hearing the coarse insults which were sent after her. She entered the play-ground, where she was saluted with more remarks of the same sort, not addressed directly to her, but passing from one to the other.

"Here comes my lady's pet, the witch!" "See the fine scholar, who can get her own lace made while she spoils other folks' work!"

Isabel took refuge in the school-room; but even here she was not safe.

"Don't you go in there till mistress comes!" she heard Peggy say to one of the children.

"Why not? I want Isabel to help me to learn my lesson!"

"Don't you speak to Isabel! Don't you know she will put a spell upon you, and make you grow crooked and pine away, as poor little Franky Corbet did!"

"I don't believe it!" said the little girl; but nevertheless she did not enter the schoolroom. Isabel laid her head down on her desk, and prayed with all her heart for grace to forgive and to endure. As she did so, a strange peace and quietness stole over her heart. God seemed to come very near to her, and to bring home to her the hundreds of sweet promises of his word. "I will never leave thee nor forsake thee." "My sheep hear my voice, and none are able to pluck them out of my hands." "Who shall separate us from the love of Christ?" The peace of God which passeth understanding seemed to flow in upon her in a flood. When her persecutors entered the school-room after the mistress had come, and glanced at the face of their victim, they saw something written there which they could not understand.

"How happy she looks!" whispered Cicely to Janey. "I believe she is a true Christian, if ever one lived. I wish I was like her!"

"You may be if you take the same way!" said Janey.

Another person in the room saw Isabel's peaceful face with very different feelings from Cicely's. Mabel was more miserable than ever. She knew what a mean and spiteful part she had acted. She despised and hated herself; but her self-contempt did not drive her to the Savior! It only made her hate Isabel the more, as the cause of her humiliation. What right had Isabel to look so calm, nay, so happy, when she was so miserable? Why did the color rise in Isabel's cheek and her eyes moisten when the mistress read the ninety-first psalm:—"He shall deliver thee from the snare of the fowler. He shall cover thee with his feathers, and under his wings shalt thou trust: his truth shall be thy shield and buckler. There shall no evil befall thee." "He shall call upon me, and I will answer him: I will be with him in trouble."

What were these words to Mabel? They brought no comfort to her. She would have been glad to forget God altogether if that had been possible. But Isabel seemed to think it was all written expressly for her. Afterwards, in the reading lesson, at the passage, "Blessed are ye when men shall revile you," etc., Isabel glanced at the mistress with a lovely smile, and her face seemed to glow with light. Could she be approving these words to herself? What right had Isabel to think that any thing in the Bible was written for her? Isabel was not thinking of herself, but of her mother; and Elizabeth Ellenwood rejoiced in the smile and glance, as additional evidence that the cloud had passed from the girl's soul.

Some such thoughts seemed at this moment to be passing through Jane Lee's mind, for she asked, "Please, mistress, ought we to think that any thing in the Bible is written for us?"

"Of course!" replied the mistress. "Every thing in the Bible is written for us. You know that, Jane!"

"Yes, I know," said Jane; "but—"

"Take time!" said the mistress; "tell me just what you are thinking!"

"I mean that sometimes when we are reading we find a verse which seems as if it were just made for us, and I want to know if it is right to take it to ourselves."

"Certainly it is right. That is the way in which God's saints of all ages have found comfort. The Scriptures are made for sinning and suffering men and women, and it is natural to expect there will be something in them to suit every particular case." After a pause she added, "God's promises are made for all his saints, and his threatenings for all who willfully go on in sin and set at naught his goodness!"

Could the mistress have meant those words for her? Mabel asked herself. Was she going on willfully in sin and setting at naught God's goodness! She knew that she was; but she was not prepared to acknowledge her sin. No! whatever it cost her, she would not humble herself to Isabel!

Everyday Isabel found her walk to school growing more and more unpleasant. In vain did she go earlier than any of the others. Somebody was always watching

her. If she ventured into the play-ground, she met with
nothing but open or overt abuse and insulting allusions to
her mother; nor was she secure in the school-room. None
of the girls now held any conversation with her but the
Lees and Penbuthys and Cicely Hurd, and even the twins
looked rather askance at her.

"Where is Isabel, dame?" asked Jan Lee, one afternoon,
entering the "house place" at the Red House, where Dame
Winne was busy with her spinning.

"At the school," replied Dame Winne, "unless she
has stopped behind to help the mistress with the work!
Mistress is very fond of her!"

"And well she may be, for a sweeter maid never
breathed!" said Jan, with emphasis. "My dame loves her
like a daughter. But, dame, do you know what tales are
passing in the village about the poor child?"

Dame Winne had heard nothing. She seldom stirred
over the threshold of her own door, save to go to church or
to visit some sick neighbor; and we all know that when a
scandal is afloat, the persons most concerned are generally the last to hear of it. As she heard Jan's tale, she first
cried and wrung her hands, and then grew indignant.

"But who could have told the story at all?" she asked.
"Nobody knows it here save our two selves and the mistress. I was sorry that Isabel told her; but I am sure *she*
would not tattle."

"Not she!" said Jan, with emphasis. "I would trust her
with the secret which concerned my life. Anyhow the tale
is out, and my maid Jane says that it is thrown in Isabel's
face every day, and that she never goes to school without
being insulted. I am afraid it will come to worse before we
hear the last of it!"

Dame Winne turned pale.

"What shall we do?" she said. "Oh, who could be so
cruel to my poor orphan maid?"

"That I cannot tell for certain," replied Jan. "But it will
all come out to the light: *that* you may be sure. I thought

of speaking to the mistress, for Janey says she knows nothing about the matter; but I would do nothing in the business till I saw you and Master Jasper. Where is he?"

"He has gone up to Millheads with the barley."

"Then I'll tell you what, dame! Do you go with me to see mistress, and we will lay the whole matter before her. 'Tis a fine day, and you can take your time!"

The dame put on her out-of-door dress, the mufflers and peaked hat, the red cloak and high clogs, which she had worn ever since her marriage, and set out with the good fisherman for the cottage of the mistress. As they drew near the end of the lane which opened upon the village green, they heard a confused noise of shouts and laughter, which explained itself as they came out from behind the group of hawthorn trees which partly concealed the gate. There was Isabel in the middle of a group of boys and girls, who surrounded her so completely, that she could not get away from them, while they shouted every sort of coarse taunt and insult in her ears. Chief among her tormentors and close to the dame and Jasper, stood Peggy Hollins, cheering on the others.

"Give it to her!" she called. "Let's see if her mother will come on a broomstick and carry her away!" and she concluded with a loud laugh at her own wit. Her merriment was disagreeably interrupted. Dame Winne had hobbled quickly forward, and before the laugh was out of her mouth, Peggy received a box on the ear which made her head ring more chimes than the church bells on the king's birthday.

"So it is thou who hast brought up an evil report on my maid!" said the Dame, almost out of breath. "Thou whom I have fed when thou hadst never a morsel to put between thee and starving! I'll teach thee to tell lies, thou mischievous minx!" and again the cuff was repeated, with more emphasis than before. Peggy blubbered, and the ring of boys became silent, apparently undecided whether to show fight or run away. But a new actor now appeared upon the scene, which inclined most of them to the latter course.

"Why do you beat the poor girl, dame!" said a gentle voice: and Lady Stantoun came round the corner of the churchyard, attended by Mrs. Brewster and a man with a basket. "What has she done?"

"She has told lies about my poor maid, my lady," returned Dame Winne, her respect for "the quality" giving away to her grief and anger. "She has miscalled her for a witch, and has set the boys and girls on to abuse and maltreat her. Look at her, my lady, all covered with mud, and her poor neck and arms bruised and bleeding, with the stones thrown at her. Tell me what this minx deserves for her pains!"

"'Twasn't me alone, and I didn't begin it, either!" blubbered Peggy. "I never should have thought of it but for Mabel Winne. If Isabel isn't a witch, it was her own cousin that said so,—ay, and that told the story about her mother, to boot! So there, Dame Winne!"

"Mabel! no, thou liar! My Mabel never did such a thing!" said the dame. "She would scorn it. 'Tis your own wickedness, and none of Mabel's doings."

"You may ask the other maids, then!" said Peggy, sullenly.

"I fear she tells the truth this time, Dame Winne!" said Jan Lee. "My Janey said the same thing,—that Mabel had begun it, and that it was she who had told the tale about Isabel's mother."

"This is a grave matter!" said Lady Stantoun. "It must be examined into with care. Are you well advised of what you say, Master Lee!"

"My Janey never told a lie in her life, my lady!" replied Jan, with flattering pride. "The mistress will tell you the same!"

"I know well that Janey is a very good girl!" replied Lady Stantoun, smiling. "But Mabel has heretofore borne a good character also, and we must not condemn her unheard. I pray you, my good Dame Winne, leave this matter in my hands. I will see that justice is done on all sides, to the guilty as well as the innocent!" And Lady Stantoun turned her eyes round upon the throng of boys and girls, with a look which made some of them wish themselves at Sandy Island, or even further away! "Tomorrow I will myself come down to the school, and we will then know the whole story."

Dame Winne curtseyed, and murmured blessings and thanks for the condescension and goodness of her lady. As Lady Stantoun moved away, Jan followed her a few steps, and she turned with her usual kindness to hear what he had to say.

"If you please, my lady, what shall we do with Isabel tonight? I very much fear she will not be safe at home with only the old people!"

"Surely matters cannot have gone so far as that!" said Lady Stantoun.

"There is no saying, madam!" replied Jan. "We have enough spirits here ripe for any villainy, and ready to welcome a chance for burning the Red House and plundering Master Jasper. I greatly fear there will be mischief before morning!"

"Halloo, what is all this?" cried a cheery voice: and Lord Stantoun rode up, followed by his groom and huntsman. "What have you said to my lady, Jan Lee, to turn her so pale?"

Jan had played with Lord Stantoun as a boy, and stood by no means so much in awe of him as of his lady. He briefly repeated the story of what had happened, and his fears of violence to the old people and their adopted child.

Lord Stantoun was a man of no very fixed principles; but he was brave and generous, with that sort of disposition which sides with the weaker party, right or wrong. He well knew his own power, for besides that he was a magistrate, the lords of Stantoun Court had been a kind of kings on their own estates for many generations. He swore it was a burning shame, and he would put a stop to it.

"Do you, Jan, and your sons act as guard at the Red House, with as many of the fisher lads as you will need, and spare neither dry blows nor powder in case these fellows attempt mischief. I will send you ammunition and refreshments from the Court. Let the old people and the child come up to the great house if they will. No one shall touch a hair of their head while I am able to prevent it. Stay, I will read them a lesson." And, spurring his horse into the midst of the crowd which had collected on the green, he delivered to them, with sufficiently energetic tones and words, his opinion of their conduct, reminding them at the last that their leases would soon need renewing, and that most of them were mere tenants at will, and declaring that he would turn out every man, woman, and child who should engage in another such affair as that of Madam Corbet had been!

"There has been enough of this folly," he added,— "enough of drowning old women and burning young ones. Let me hear any more of it, and I will be worse to you than all the witches between here and Trent. So beware!"

The interference of Lord and Lady Stantoun had already produced a change in the face of affairs. The very parents who had set on their young ones to abuse and revile Isabel, now began to believe in her innocence, and to think that there could be nothing bad about a girl whose part was so vigorously taken by the Earl and Countess. When Peggy Hollins returned home she was greeted with a storm of abuse from her mother, ending with,—

"You will never rest till you get us turned out of house and home by your tricks. Why need *you* meddle in the matter? I should not wonder if my lady turned you out of the school for all you have done!"

Peggy was not without her own fears of the same sort; nor was she the only one who entertained them. A good many of the girls would have given their best ribbons to undo what they had done during the last week. The disposition was general to throw all the blame upon Mabel.

"I am sure I, for one, should never have thought of blaming Isabel, if Mabel had not begun about it." "I thought she was a very nice girl till Mabel began to hint about her, and I thought 'To be sure she must know, as Isabel is her cousin.'" Such were some of the remarks made as the girls gathered in the play-ground before school.

Mabel had seen the beginning of the affray the day before; but she had hurried away long before its close, and as her home was nearly a mile from the village, she had heard nothing of Lady Stantoun's interference. She came to school next morning before the bell was rung, wishing and hoping she hardly knew what; nor did she know whether to feel relieved or disappointed when she saw Isabel in her usual seat, pale, indeed, but calm and serene as ever. She did not know how to read the glances the girls cast at her, nor the looks bent upon her by the mistress. The one expressed sorrow and reproof, the others anger and scorn; and it was with a feeling of uncomfortable foreboding that she took her place. After the opening exercises were finished, she arose, as usual, to distribute the books and work.

"Stay, Mabel!" said the mistress. "You can keep your seat. We shall have no lessons just at present!"

Mabel resumed her seat, and the girls sat silent, and unemployed, wondering what was to come next, and some of them wishing themselves anywhere else than in Lady Rosamond's school. Never since the room was built had a more uncomfortable half hour been passed within its walls. At the end of that time the door opened, and Lady Stantoun, attended by Doctor Parnell and followed by Mrs. Brewster, walked up between the rows of desks, and took her place upon the platform at the upper end of the room, where the mistress usually sat.

"I have come, girls," said she, in a distinct, impressive voice, which was heard in every corner of the room, "to try to learn something of the cause and beginning of the disgraceful scene which occurred upon the village green yesterday. I learned then that a shameful charge had been thrown on one of your number—upon an orphan stranger!" she said, with an emphasis which went to more than one heart, "and a scholar who has appeared to me one of the best in the school. I saw this schoolmate of yours just after she had been grossly insulted, and I saw a number of those before me engaged, as it seemed, in helping on the attack."

She was silent, and stood for a moment looking all over the school. Then she said, in a commanding voice, "Peggy Hollins, Anne Davis, Mary Styles, Judith and Joan Hawtree, stand up in your places!"

There was no help for it, and the girls arose, feeling as if they had been called to execution.

"Peggy Hollins, how did you hear first this story that Isabel was a witch? Speak the truth, or it will be a great deal worse for you!"

"It was Mabel Winne, so it was, my lady!" whimpered Peggy. "I am sure I never thought of such a thing before she said it, and the other girls will tell you the same!"

"Mabel Winne!" exclaimed Lady Stantoun; and the doctor ejaculated, "Impossible, my lady! Mabel Winne is head girl, and has borne a high character for years. This wretched girl is only seeking to shift the blame from her own shoulders."

"Peggy, you will gain nothing by any such course!" said Lady Stantoun. "Tell me the truth."

"You may ask any of the girls: they all heard her!" said Peggy, sullenly. "It wasn't me more than any of the rest of them."

"Can it be possible that Mabel has set on these persecutions?" asked the lady, in a low voice, turning to the mistress. "How shall I get at the truth?"

"Let us hear what the others have to say," suggested Doctor Parnell.

"LADY STANTON TOOK HER PLACE UPON THE PLATFORM
AT THE UPPER END OF THE ROOM."

Lady Stantoun questioned the other culprits; but their stories all agreed, and pointed to Mabel as the beginner of the mischief.

"Who first told the tale of Isabel's family misfortunes?" asked Lady Stantoun.

"Please, my lady, it was Mabel!" answered Mary. "She told it in the play-ground, the Monday after holidays."

The other girls were questioned, and all agreed in the same story.

"Is this true, Mabel?" asked Lady Stantoun.

Mabel was silent at first; but on the question being repeated, she replied, "It is true that I told the story of Isabel's mother."

"And is it true you were the first to throw this odious accusation upon Isabel!"

Mabel was silent.

"How shall I get at the truth concerning this matter?" repeated Lady Stantoun, turning to the mistress again. "Is there one of these girls who can be depended upon to relate the circumstances as they occurred?"

"Yes, my lady!" replied the mistress. "I think you may depend upon the word of Jane Lee, or that of Cicely Hurd, or Ellen Penbuthy. I have never found either of them out in a lie, and Jane especially is very exact and careful in all she says."

"Jane Lee, stand up, and tell me all you know of this matter from first to last."

Janey arose, and repeated the whole story, from Mabel's first insinuations as to the cause of Isabel's success in lace-making to the last open accusations. The other girls confirmed her story, and Cicely added that Mabel had said that Isabel had enticed little Patience out on the cliff in the first place.

"Mabel, how did you hear the story of Isabel's mother?" asked the lady.

"Isabel herself told me!" replied Mabel.

She had not intended to tell this lie a moment before;

but it was out now, and there was no help for it. She must stand by what she had said: so she thought, and a hard feeling of recklessness took possession of her.

"Is this true Isabel? Did you tell Mabel?"

"No, my lady!" replied Isabel. "I never told anybody but the mistress till after Mabel spoke of it in the playground. Then I told the girls that what she said was true."

Mabel, however, persisted in the statement that Isabel had told her, and Lady Stantoun almost began to believe that Isabel might have let the secret slip out unawares, when light was thrown upon the subject from an unexpected quarter. Little Patience, sitting with "the babes" in the front row, fancied that Isabel was being blamed unjustly, and, in her eagerness to defend her friend, she forgot all rules, and spoke up eagerly.

"Please, my lady! Cicely Hurd knows how Mabel heard the story!"

"Hush, Patience!" said the mistress. "Do not speak before you are spoken to?"

"We will forgive her this time!" said Lady Stantoun. "Is it true, Cicely, that you can throw any light upon this matter?"

"I believe I can, my lady; but I promised Isabel that I would not say any thing unless I was asked," replied Cicely. She had been sitting on thorns for some minutes, and now inwardly promised Patience the biggest apple in her father's orchard as a reward for her well-timed interference.

"Let me hear what you have to say, then; and be careful to speak no more than you know of your own knowledge."

"I was sitting by the window in our garret picking wool, my lady!" began Cicely. "It was last Saturday was a week, in the afternoon, and the mistress was busy at work in the arbor in her garden. I saw Isabel come in with a bundle and some books in her hands, and she and mistress went into the house. Presently I saw Mabel come in with a basket, as though she was going to the garden gate. As she came under the casement, which was open, she stopped, and stood there for a full half-hour as still as a stone, till mistress and Isabel came out of the house again."

"How did you know the time?" asked Doctor Parnell.

"Because the church clock struck four just as she came in, and it was the half-hour as the mistress came out of the house!"

"Was that the time when Isabel told you her story?" asked Lady Stantoun, turning to the mistress.

"It was, my lady!" replied Elizabeth, who saw herself obliged, however unwillingly, to believe Cicely's story. "The idea occurred to my own mind, as I saw Mabel among the bushes, that she had been listening; but I was unwilling to believe it. I have always been very fond of Mabel," she added, in a voice which trembled a little. "I believed her worthy of confidence in every respect. I was surprised to perceive, soon after Isabel came here, that Mabel had taken a dislike to her cousin; but I thought it no more than a fancy, which would soon pass by!"

"Have you had any complaint to make of Isabel?" asked the lady.

"None whatever! Her conduct has been faultless, so far as I have seen her. She is rather slow at learning in every respect except where dexterity of hands and patience is required, as in needle-work and lace-making; but she is painstaking and industrious."

"Have you heard any thing of these stories of witchcraft?"

"Never till yesterday, my lady! I have always trusted Mabel to keep order in the play-ground, and I have never encouraged the girls to come to me with tales of each other, and have used all my influence to discredit the stories of witchcraft and the like, which are, unfortunately, too common among us!"

Lady Stantoun asked a few more questions and then sat down, while Doctor Parnell arose to speak to the girls. It was a failing of the excellent parson (for excellent he was in every respect) that he sometimes seemed to write his sermons rather for his own mind than for that of his flock, and used more large words and more Greek and Latin quotations than were altogether to the edification of a rural congregation; but no one could say that he did not on this occasion speak with sufficient plainness. He set before his auditors, in the most feeling and forcible manner, the meanness and cruelty of which they had been guilty in thus slandering and persecuting an innocent girl, who had never harmed one of them, but who, by their own showing, was ready to help them on every occasion. He spoke of the woes denounced against those who oppress the stranger and the fatherless, and who are guilty of slander and mischief-making. He showed them their folly in believing for a moment the idle tales they had heard, and concluded by advising them to put away all anger and malice from their hearts, to believe in God and to serve him. If they did these things, neither Satan nor any of his servants could do them harm. "For believe me, my maids," he concluded, "when you lend yourself to do the work of the devil in leading others astray, and tempting them, either by persecution or persuasion, to sin against God, you are his servants, and in his power as entirely as the rankest witch that ever lived—supposing that there ever was such a thing!"

There was a short consultation among the elders, and then the punishment of the offenders was announced. Four or five of the principal culprits, with Mabel and Peggy at their head, were to be suspended from the school and its privileges for three weeks—a punishment which their parents were likely to make sufficiently severe. Mabel was degraded from her place as head girl to the foot of the class to which she belonged (her place being taken by Jane Lee, the next in age and standing), and ordered publicly to beg Isabel's pardon.

"And now, Isabel, what shall I do for you, to make amends for the treatment you have received in my school?" asked Lady Stantoun.

"Please, my lady, I need no amends!" replied Isabel; "but oh, my lady, if I might only beg one favor!"

"Well!" said Lady Stantoun, smiling. "It must be something very unreasonable if I do not grant it you. Speak without any fear!"

"If you would only forgive the girls and Mabel, my lady! I am sure they meant no such great harm. They did not think to what it would grow; and you know," she added, sorrowfully, "such things have befallen better people than me, and even in this very town! The girls hear such things talked of by their elders, and it is no wonder they believe what they hear!"

"That is true, to our shame be it spoken!" remarked the doctor. "If my people had half as much fear of God as they have of witches, pixys, and moormen, I should have more hope of them! I think, my lady, considering the good character which Mabel Winne has hitherto borne, she might be forgiven on her making submission. As to Peggy Hollins and those Hawtrees!" he added, in a lower tone, "it were well if the school were rid of them altogether!"

"Let it be so!" replied Lady Stantoun, after consulting the mistress. "Isabel's request is granted so far as this. Mabel shall be forgiven and allowed to attend school, on her asking pardon of the mistress and of Isabel; but she shall be removed from her place as head girl, for which she has shown herself unfit. The other girls shall be put upon a month's probation, during which time they shall have no play hours, and they shall have extra tasks in spinning and knitting. If at the end of that time there is no farther complaint of them, they shall be restored to their former places,—always provided that they beg pardon, as aforesaid, of the mistress and of Isabel."

Isabel would have liked to see the girls fully pardoned; but she had the tact to perceive that she had better say no more, so she made her reverence to Lady Stantoun and sat down. At a sign from the doctor, each of the condemned ones arose in her place, and, in words detailed by him, begged pardon, beginning with the youngest.

"Now, Mabel!" said he at last. But Mabel sat still, and would neither move nor speak.

"Mabel, my child!" said the mistress. "Pray, do not be obstinate; only show by your words and your subsequent conduct that you are truly sorry, and all will be soon forgotten!"

Mabel would not move, and her face assumed a hard expression.

"I cannot recede from what I have said, Mabel!" said Lady Stantoun. "You must comply with the conditions I have laid down or leave the school! No, Isabel, not another word!" she added, meeting Isabel's imploring glances. "It becomes Mabel to set an example in this respect, as she should have done in others!"

"I will never beg Isabel's pardon!" said Mabel, her passion getting the upperhand. "Never, if I die for it! It is all her fault,—all! She got me into disgrace the very first day she came to school, and she has stood in my way ever since. I hate her! and I will never forgive her, much less ask her forgiveness!"

There was an awful pause. The girls looked as if they expected the roof to fall in, and crush the presumptuous one who had answered Lady Stantoun back in her own school-room. Isabel looked more disturbed than she had ever done in the days of her persecution. At last Lady Stantoun spoke.

"Mabel, take your cloak and hood and go home, and never let me see you here again till you are prepared to humble yourself and take the lowest place."

Trembling with anger and excitement, Mabel rose to obey. She was unexpectedly hindered. Isabel could bear it no longer. Bursting into tears and holding Mabel by the cloak, she tried to detain her, while she sobbed, "Oh, my lady! wait a little! Give her a little time! Mabel, Mabel! Think what your father and mother will say!"

But Isabel's intervention only increased her cousin's

anger. Mabel pushed her aside with violence which almost threw her down. Then, making a mocking courtesy to my lady, she left the room, shutting the door with violence.

CHAPTER VIII

ON THE CLIFF

As soon as school was out, the girls began to gather about Isabel, who was still crying bitterly, some trying to console her, some anxious to excuse themselves.

"Oh, yes! it was Mabel, all Mabel, of course, and nobody else was in fault!" said Jane Lee, contemptuously, in answer to some such remarks. "Easy to lay it all to Mabel, now that she is in disgrace!"

"Well, Janey, you said yourself that she began it!" remarked Mary Styles.

"So she did; but what then? Had you not eyes and ears of your own? Were you obliged to agree with her in every thing, and to persecute the innocent because she bade you? You have never been so ready to follow her lead in other things, to learn your lessons, and mind your stops, and keep yourselves neat and clean, because Mabel told you to, or because she did these things? I'll tell you what! I should think a good deal better of you if you were more ready to take shame to yourselves and less prompt to trample on the fallen. I never have much hope of anybody's penitence who makes out that it was all the fault of somebody else."

"You are right, Janey!" said Judith Hawtree, very unexpectedly,—for she was one of the worst girls in the school. "For my part, I am free to take all the shame to myself, and to say that we have got less than we deserved: *that* we have; and we ought to be thankful for getting off so well. I have been a bad girl, and I mean to do better. It shall go hard; but I will show that I am in earnest. And so, Isabel, I beg your pardon again, and I am sorry I ever said or did one thing to hurt you."

"Well done, Judith!" exclaimed Jane and Cicely together. "That is talking like a brave honest maid!" added Jane. "I am sure Isabel does forgive you; don't you, dear!"

"Indeed I do!" replied Isabel, kissing Judith heartily. "I have said all the time it was more a mistake than any thing else."

"You *are* a good little thing!" said Judith's sister Joan. "I take shame to myself, too, that I ever thought otherwise. I felt all the time parson was talking as if I should like to creep into a crab-shell!"

"It would be a good-sized crab, then!" said Isabel, unable to forbear a smile, for Joan was the fattest girl in school. "But let us say no more about the matter; only, dear girls, *do* try to love God and to serve him, and then you will not be afraid of any terror by night or by day!"

"Isabel, have you seen my Mabel?" said Mabel's mother, coming into the house-place at the Red House late in the day. "She is not here, is she?" The poor woman's manner was full of anxiety, and her eyes red with weeping.

"No; I have not seen her since this morning, when she left the school-room," replied Isabel, starting. "Has she not been at home?"

"No," replied the poor woman, bursting into tears; "nor would it do any good if she had. Her father has been to the mistress and heard the whole story from her, and he declares that Mabel shall never enter his doors again till she makes submission!"

"Surely that is hard on the poor maid!" said Jasper Winne: "that her own father should turn against her. Whatever she has done, her father's door should not be shut against her!"

"You know what John is!" said Dame Winne. "Once he sets his foot down, nobody can move him. I wish thee no harm, Isabel, nor do I blame thee; but it is hard to have my Mabel's path crossed and her home shut against her all because of thee!"

"But, Anne, you must not be hard upon Isabel neither!" said Jasper, restraining his wife, who was ready to take up arms in defense of "her maid." "As far as I can learn, Isabel did her best to beg Mabel off. And more than that, you should remember that Isabel bore all Mabel's unkindness in silence. She never told the mistress nor us what she had to put up with; and but for Jan Lee we should perhaps not have known one word of the business till the poor girl was murdered outright."

"I know, I know. But oh, Jasper, if even you bore a kindness to me or mine, take in the poor willful maid, and give her shelter till she shall come to a better mind. She hath far too much of her father's temper, and I fear what will come of this disgrace."

"That will I, Anne!" said the old man, heartily. "You know I have always loved Mabel, and I will never see her want. Can you give a guess, Isabel, where your cousin can be?"

"Isabel is not here!" said his wife. "She just slipped out. I dare say she has gone to seek Mabel. I wish she would not venture outside the gate. I am afraid for her! and there is a storm rising too."

"Never you fear!" said the old man, shrewdly. "The children, both boys and girls, have had their lesson, and none of the men will meddle with my lady's favorite so long as my lord is at hand. But I will go out and seek the maids, for it is too late for them to be abroad."

Isabel had indeed gone out to seek Mabel, and persuade her to come home to her uncle's house. She asked more than one person without receiving any information. At last a school-boy told her that he had seen Mabel walking along on the top of the cliff. Isabel's heart sunk at the news, and, fearing she knew not what, she hurried along the path which Mabel had taken. She had gone fully a half mile, and was quite beyond the precincts of the village, when, in the gathering twilight, she discovered Mabel sitting on a stone, resting her elbow on her knee and her chin on her hands.

"Thank God, she is at least safe!" thought Isabel, with a sigh of relief. Then, after a moment's pause, she went up to Mabel and laid her hand on her shoulder.

"Dear Mabel! do not sit here in the dew," said she, trying to speak as usual. "It is growing late, and there is a storm coming up. Uncle Jasper wishes you to come to our house. Your mother is there, and waits to see you."

Mabel started, as if stung by a snake, and threw off Isabel's hand; but she did not speak.

"Do come, Mabel!" urged Isabel, kneeling beside her, heedless that she was on the very verge of the cliff. "Only hear the thunder. You will be wet through, and your mother is so unhappy about you. No one will say an unkind word to you. Nobody desires to do so, I am sure."

"I will not come!" said Mabel, passionately. "I will not go to your house to be pitied and looked down on by you. Enjoy your triumph and let me alone."

"But, Mabel, you cannot stay here all night!"

"What is it to you where I stay—or to anybody!" added Mabel, bursting into tears. "Who cares what becomes of me? Who would care if I were down there in the sea?"

"God!" said Isabel, solemnly. "Oh, Mabel, only go to Him and all will yet be well! Do come, Mabel! How can I go home without you?"

"Go where you will," she exclaimed, "but leave me alone!"

Suddenly she stopped. She was alone indeed. Where was Isabel? Had she vanished into air? What had set that stone falling from point to point of the cliff? What had roused the gulls from their nests and sent them swarming out to seaward? What was the meaning of that crumbled turf at the edge of the cliff? Starting suddenly back at the violence of Mabel's gesticulations, Isabel had lost her footing, and was nowhere to be seen.

Mabel stood for a moment as if turned into stone. Then she turned and ran towards the village, filling the air with her screams. It seemed an age before she reached the first house and roused the inmates, already asleep at the early hour of eight.

"What is it, my maid? What has happened?" asked Jan Lee, who was hastening homeward, to avoid the rapidly gathering storm.

"Isabel! she has fallen over the cliff by the White Rock. Oh, Master Lee, Isabel is killed!"

"Nay, that she is for certain, if she has fallen over there," said an old man. "I mind when my pony——"

"Don't stand prating about ponies!" exclaimed Jan Lee, recovering his senses, which had been as it were suspended by Mabel's news, "but let us think what can be done. Some one run and ring the church bells. Get lanterns, torches, and the ropes, and follow me. At least let us find the poor maid's body before the tide sweeps it out to sea, though I fear we can do little, with this wind rising."

"How came Isabel at the White Rock?" asked somebody.

"She came to find me," answered Mabel, but, overwrought in mind and body, she could say no more. Sight and sense failed, and she sank down in a deadly swoon. When she recovered, she found herself lying on the mistress's bed, while Elizabeth herself was attending on her.

"Isabel!" she exclaimed, starting up, "have they found her?"

"Not yet. They can do nothing tonight. The wind blows so that no one can go down the cliff, or even keep a light. Lie still, Mabel. You are not fit to stir. See, your head turns as soon as you rise."

Mabel had indeed sunk back with a groan. "But she *must* be found!" she said, wildly. "She must be found, or I shall go after her. Mistress, it was all my fault!"

"Hush, hush, Mabel! These are wild words."

"It was!" repeated Mabel. "I frightened her by my violence, and she fell over the cliff!"

"My child, you know not what you say. All will be done for poor Isabel that is possible. Let me hear not a word more tonight. Tomorrow you shall tell me what you will."

There was no help for it, and Mabel lay still—so still
that the mistress thought her asleep; and, wearied by the
events of the day, she slept too, leaning back in her great
chair. But Mabel was not sleeping. She was going over and
over in her mind all the events of the last three months—
over all her intercourse with Isabel from that first day of
the school-feast to this last evening. She had begun by a
vague distrust and jealousy of Isabel from the first day.
She fancied that Isabel would usurp her place in the affec-
tions of her uncle and aunt, and deprive her of the inheri-
tance which she had learned to look upon as her right.
That was the beginning. Then she had been displeased
with the attention paid by the mistress to the stranger,
and by the admiration which the girls had expressed for
her. She had disliked Isabel from the moment that her
own neglect and rudeness had drawn upon her the notice
of Lady Stantoun. From that day she had watched her
cousin with a jealous and envious eye. Isabel's growing favor with the mistress, her kindness to the little ones and
her influence over them, her decided preference of Jane
Lee rather than herself for an intimate friend,—though
she well knew that she had repelled all Isabel's advances,—her unexpected success in the lace-making, and the
notice which she had received from Lady Stantoun in consequence,—all had helped to feed and nourish the "bitter root" of envy, till it had borne its legitimate fruit of
unkindness, slander, and persecution, and now perhaps
death. And what had Isabel done, after all? Nothing! She
had returned good for evil in every case. Not so much as
an unkind word had ever escaped her lips. Well, Isabel
was in heaven now! That was one comfort. No one could
hurt her any more. She had loved God, and she had gone
to him. Mabel shuddered as she recalled her own last
words to herself.

Mabel no longer excused herself—no longer justified herself in her own eyes. She now, for the first time,
saw herself just as she was. She saw what her former

self-righteousness had amounted to, and she abhorred and loathed herself. She saw that she had never loved God or thought of serving and pleasing him. Her good deeds had been done only to be seen by men, and her desire of becoming a saint had been founded not on that love and devotion to God which forgets itself, and is content to be known only to him, but on vanity, pride, vainglory, and hypocrisy,—a desire to take the highest room at the feast and to have praise of men. All her virtues had been like the play-gardens the little children made in the sand, gay indeed, and even fragrant, but withering and corrupting in the first blast of wind or the first ray of sunshine. She had deceived and cheated every one, and herself most of all. Only God had seen her as she really was.

Often had Mabel confessed herself a "miserable sinner," and besought God to have mercy upon her; but now for the first time she felt that she was a sinner indeed, a lost sheep, which had wandered away out of the sound of the Shepherd's voice, too far, it seemed, for any possibility of return. Her own father had cast her off, and her sins against him had been as nothing to her transgressions against her Father in heaven. No; there was no hope, no comfort, no light anywhere! All was dark, and must be so,—dark and hopeless for time and eternity.

Such were some of the thoughts which passed through Mabel's mind again and again as she lay on the mistress's bed through that long night, motionless, indeed, but wide awake, and watching the casement for the dawn, which seemed as if it would never come. At last the window began to be distinguished from the rest of the night,—

"The casement slowly grew a glimmering square,"—

and a bird chirped from the garden outside. Cautiously Mabel slipped from the bed, and glided out of the cottage like a shadow, without waking the mistress. She could see her way now well enough in the rapidly-growing twilight of the summer morning. She had not dared to put on her shoes, for fear of rousing the mistress, and the stones cut her feet; but she hardly felt them. When she found herself beyond the village, she sat down to rest, for she felt weak and giddy. She bathed her face and head with water from the leaves, and presently, feeling rested and refreshed, she walked rapidly up the path towards the cliff. There was the white stone and the place where Isabel had kneeled beside her, persuading her to come home, telling her that God cared for her misery, and loved her despite her sin. Oh, if she had but listened to the gentle pleading voice, how different would every thing have been! Then it was not too late. And then came to Mabel's mind the words she had read in school only the day before, "Whosoever hateth his brother is a murderer!"

It was broad daylight when she reached the white stone, and a golden gleam over the summit of the high moor showed where the sun would presently come up. Mabel stood a moment, and then, throwing herself down at full length upon the turf, she strained her eyes to gaze over the edge of the cliff. All was dim at first; but as her vision cleared she saw something on a narrow ledge about thirty feet below, close beside a bush growing on the scanty soil! Did it move? or was it the shimmering of her own eyes? Mabel gasped for breath, and then called, "Isabel!"

There was a motion! She was sure of it. She called again.

"Isabel! Can it be you? Oh, Isabel, if you love me, answer me!"

If there was any answer, she did not hear it; but oh, joy unspeakable! there was an unmistakable movement,— the waving of a hand and a white kerchief. Isabel was there, and alive!

"Don't move, for your life!" cried Mabel. "I will soon bring help. Keep up good courage!"

The cove was nearer than the village, and never had any creature without wings descended the path more swiftly than did Mabel. Never heeding her bare and bleeding feet, she ran over the sharp stones and shells to Jan Lee's cottage. All was still, for it was yet very early morning. Jan said afterwards that he heard Mabel's first knock; but to Mabel herself it seemed an hour before he opened the door!

"Isabel is alive!" gasped Mabel.

"My poor maid, you are beside yourself!" said the fisherman, kindly. "You do not know what you say." And indeed his only idea was that Mabel had gone distracted with excitement.

"No, no! I do know what I say!" exclaimed Mabel, seizing his hands. "I have been to the white stone and seen her. She lies on the ledge by the thorn bush which grows there; but she is alive, and she waved her kerchief. I saw her. Oh, Jan Lee, for mercy's sake lose no time! She may yet be saved."

Jan's shout brought out his own boys, and in five minutes the whole population of the cove was alive. Jan directed and ordered, and in a marvelously short time the party were at the white stone, with all the means needed for rescuing the fallen girl.

There was a pause of breathless suspense as little Jan was lowered over the ledge, while the ropes were arranged by his father and brother. Presently came up his voice, clear and distinct,—with what eagerness did Mabel drink in each word!—

"She is alive and has her senses, but is dreadfully bruised. I shall need help."

The news was generally known by this time, and almost everybody in the village was at the cliff. The business was in the best of hands, and went on as fast as was consistent with prudence and safety; but Mabel wrung her hands and stamped her foot at the delay. She resisted all the attempts of the mistress and her mother to persuade her to come home, and could hardly be withheld from trying herself to descend the cliff. At last all was ready, and the bystanders held their breath as the ropes were drawn up, and the arm chair in which Isabel was carefully secured became visible above the edge of the precipice. Then indeed a cheer arose upon the morning air which was heard at the village!

Carefully Isabel was untied and laid upon the litter prepared for her. It was evident that she was severely hurt; but she was quite sensible, and faintly thanked those who waited on her.

"Mabel! Where is Mabel?" she asked, anxiously looking round. "Where is Mabel? It was she who found me first! Mabel saved me!"

What a pang these generous words sent through Mabel's heart. She could not speak, but she knelt beside Isabel.

"Kiss me, Mabel!" said Isabel, and as Mabel put her face down she whispered, "Oh, Mabel, try to forgive me and love me. Indeed, I never meant to do you any harm!"

It was too much. Mabel burst into a passionate fit of hysterical sobs. She was tenderly drawn away from Isabel's side by the mistress.

"Come home with me, my dear!" said Elizabeth.

"No, no! Let me go with Isabel!" sobbed Mabel.

"Yes, please, mistress!" pleaded Isabel's faint voice. "Let Mabel go home with me!"

By the thoughtfulness of Doctor Parnell, an express had been sent off to Biddeford for medical aid, the moment Isabel was discovered to be alive, and the surgeon was at hand. He pronounced Isabel's hurts to be severe and dangerous, but said that, with care, she might recover some degree of health, though she would probably remain a cripple for life. A cripple for life! Mabel shuddered as she heard it. Was there, then, to be no end to her punishment, even in this world? Had she injured her cousin beyond remedy? Oh, could she only live over the last three months! Could she only take all the suffering upon herself!

All that summer Mabel devoted herself to Isabel. She was never weary of waiting upon her, night or day, and could hardly be prevailed upon to take sufficient food and sleep. It was wonderful to see the change in the proud, willful girl. No office was too lowly for her to perform, no fatigue too great for her to endure. When, after many weary months, Isabel left her bed and her darkened room, Mabel was still at her side, reading to her, helping her in every way, and unwearied in seeking what could divert or please the languid invalid. Everyone talked of her presence and her devotion to her cousin, and if Mabel had still made human praise the object of her ambition, she might have had her fill; but Mabel cared no more for the praise of man. What was it to her that her father forgave her, that Lady Stantoun spoke kindly to her, that her aunt praised her good qualities as nurse? what was it even that Isabel loved her, and could hardly bear to let her be away an hour, so long as a dark heavy cloud was spread between her soul and Heaven, and she felt the wrath of God abiding on her? What was it that Doctor Parnell gave her his blessing, so long as the blessing of God was withheld?—so long as all her self-denial, all her prayers brought her no peace?

"Will you come out to the garden, Mabel?" asked Isabel, one lovely October day. "I feel so strong and well this morning, I should like to sit in the arbor a little while."

Isabel's least wish was law; and Mabel supported her feeble steps to the easy seat, which Master Jasper had made purposely for her.

"How lovely every thing is!" said Isabel, as she looked around her. "I think this world was never so beautiful before."

"You have been shut up so long!" said Mabel.

"Yes; it is partly that, but not altogether. I am so happy, that it makes every thing seem full of joy. When I first came here, it seemed to me that I could never be happy again!"

"'Tis no wonder, considering how you were treated!" said Mabel.

"It was not that!" replied Isabel. "Many people were kind to me even then; but my own mind was all dark. I seemed shut up to myself, groping in darkness, unable to find God anywhere. It was that which made me miserable. I had loved and trusted him, and it seemed to me that he had disappointed and deserted me in my need."

"I do not wonder you were sad!" said Mabel. "It seems to me that if I did not think him just and true, I should be more miserable than I am now, if that were possible."

"But, dear Mabel, why will you still be so unhappy?" asked Isabel. "All the trouble is over now, and why distress yourself so about what is past?"

"Because God requireth that which is past!" returned Mabel,—"because I have sinned beyond hope of pardon. My debt can never be paid, and must sink me lower and lower forever!"

"But, Mabel!" Isabel began.

"I tell you it can never be paid!" interrupted Mabel, almost fiercely. "You little know what my life has been of late,—how I have fasted and prayed and striven. All is in vain! I can never make atonement for what I have done. Even if I should repent as bitterly as King David, I should never know that my penitence was deep enough or that it was accepted. My tears can never wash away my sin. I was a persecutor of one of God's children. I see no help!"

"So was Saul of Tarsus a persecutor of God's children!" said Isabel, softly. "He was even consenting to the death of Saint Stephen, and he went to Damascus with his mind full of hate to the disciples. Yet he was forgiven, and lived and died full of hope and love!"

"Yes; but his repentance was different from mine," said Mabel.

"Was it his repentance that saved him?" asked Isabel.

"Why, yes, I suppose so!"

"I do not think so, Mabel. It was the love of God in

Christ Jesus which saved him. It was our Lord's bearing our sins in his own body on the tree, just as he bore yours and mine, dear Mabel: for God laid on him the iniquity of us all! Mabel, your own tears can never wash out one bit of your sin, though you were to weep as many drops as have fallen from Freshwater since the world was made. Your own repentance can never atone for your sin, though it were greater than that of all the forgiven sinners now in glory."

"That is what I say!" replied Mabel. "I can do nothing!"

"Yes; there is one thing which you can do!" said Isabel, with energy. "Yes, dear Mabel! *one.* You can lay aside all thought of saving yourself, and throw yourself, in all your sin and weakness, upon the mercy of God in Jesus Christ. He has made, by his own oblation of himself once offered, a full, perfect, and sufficient atonement for the sins of the whole world. He bore our sins in his own body on the tree. He has satisfied all our debt—every farthing. He has paid the ransom; and all we have to do is to come to him just as we are, to believe in his mercy, and this ransom is ours. 'Therefore, being justified by faith, we have peace with God, through our Lord Jesus Christ.'"

Isabel paused; but her heart ascended in fervent prayer for a blessing. She could hardly tell whether Mabel were listening or not. Presently she said,—

"Do you mean, Isabel, that when our Lord died on the cross he died for *me?*"

"Surely, dear maid! How could you ever doubt that?"

"And that I have nothing to do to be forgiven except to believe that he did die for me?"

"In one way you have not even to do that!" said Isabel: "that is to say, there is no merit in your doing it; but you must believe in him before you go to him. Before you will apply to the doctor, you must believe that you are sick and that the doctor can and will help you. Do you remember that day I went out on Freshwater after Patience? No; it was when you were in Langham. Well, I had got her back as far as I could, and I stretched out my other hand to get hold of the tree-root; but I could not find it. I was blind and giddy, and I believe I should have fallen, but just at that moment I caught hold of Jan Lee's hand, and then I felt myself safe at once. I had nothing to do but to give myself up and let him help me. But his holding out his hand would have done me no good if I had refused to take hold of it, and had gone on groping in darkness trying to help myself. There was no merit in my taking hold of his hand either; but it was the only thing I could do!"

"I see!" said Mabel. "But, Isabel, how can I have the face to ask Him? I am such a sinner! It is not only what I have done, but what I am doing all the time. I am just as bad as ever in my heart. I do not feel that to be one bit better than it was last summer."

"And it will never be better as you go on now!" said Isabel. "If you could make yourself good, you would have no need of Him nor of the Holy Spirit to help you. If you wait to be good before you come, you will not come at all. If I had waited on the cliff till I could find a foothold for myself, I should have gone to the bottom of Dobby's pool, and taken Patience with me!"

"Then I am to come just as I am!" said Mabel.

"That is it exactly!" replied Isabel, with animation. "Just as you are. Give up all hope or thought of any thing in yourself to deserve God's favor. You can have nothing. Ask him for forgiveness and grace, for the sake of Jesus Christ, and he will surely receive you. 'He is able to save to the *uttermost*—to the uttermost—all who come unto God by him!' 'Him that cometh to me, I will in nowise cast out!' 'Though your sins be as scarlet, they shall be as white as snow, though they be red like crimson, they shall be as wool.' All your sins, all your defilement, shall be washed away, and you shall stand before him justified by the blood of Christ! Oh Mabel, dear maid, only believe!"

"Dare I?" said Mabel. "Oh, if I might but think so! Isabel, don't deceive me with false hopes; but tell me, dare I think that he is so good as that?"

"'God so loved the world that he gave his only begotten Son, that whosoever believeth on him should not perish, but have everlasting life!'" repeated Isabel. "There is no presumption in believing his words. The presumption is in doubt!"

Slowly the light stole into Mabel's darkened mind. Gradually she saw the blessed truth that all was done,—the debt was paid, the ransom provided, the fountain opened. She had but to believe and be saved—to wash and be clean. It *was* true: she felt it; and in that moment God gave her grace to lay hold of the cross. The burden was lifted off which was crushing out her life; the thirst which was consuming her was relieved, and she was saved!

From that day life wore another face to Mabel. She saw every thing under a new light; she did every thing from a new motive. She no longer thought of herself in all she said and did. She was the servant of God, and all her work must be for him,—the soldier of Christ, and her battles were to be fought in his name and under his banner. She had much to contend with in herself, for she had by nature a warm and willful temper—which she had never learned to reduce to obedience—and a jealous disposition. But she had learned by the Spirit to mortify the deeds of the body. She had many and painful falls at first; but she learned to gather herself up again, and, seeking forgiveness and cleansing through her Savior, to go on in her way sorrowful yet always rejoicing,—sorrowful, because the harm she had caused was never undone in this world: because Isabel's few years of life were years of suffering and helplessness, which shortened her days: because her aunt and uncle early lost the adopted child who should have smoothed their own passage to the grave; rejoicing, because her sins, which were many, were forgiven for Christ's sake: because she was permitted to be the means of leading others to the same light which she had found: because she could look forward with humble confidence and steadfast hope to that land where all tears are wiped away,—where there is no more sin, neither sorrow nor crying; because all things have become new.

Isabel's life, though short, was neither useless nor unhappy. She was usually able to sit up and employ herself most of the time, and she was hardly ever idle. Her lace pillow and the embroidery, in which she learned to excel, supplied her with pleasant occupation, and with the means of relieving and comforting the poor and the sick in her neighborhood; and she had willing and discreet stewards of her bounty in Mabel and in Jane Lee. Sometimes, in fine weather, Isabel would venture as far as the school-house, supported by her friends, and such visits were holidays for all; and she often gathered the little ones around her at her own house, to teach and amuse them. She seldom went to church, but she had the comfort of many visits from good Doctor Parnell. Elizabeth Ellenwood spent many hours beside her, and Isabel was often able to give her efficient assistance in preparing work, and in helping these who needed more personal attention than the mistress could give. Yes, Isabel was very happy; and when she died, she was missed more than any one could have thought possible who had seen her life only from the outside. Even poor Peggy Hollins, in the midst of her untidiness and unthrift, was cheered and comforted by her, and shed many tears over the grave of one whom she had once persecuted almost to death.

Jane Lee continued to be head girl so long as she remained in the school. She married early and well, and lived to have one of her grandchildren called Isabel, after the friend she had loved so dearly. Her father died, respected and cherished, in extreme old age; and his descendants of the third generation loved to gather round his knees and listen to the tale of Isabel Gray and her adventures.

Elizabeth Ellenwood lived many years in Stantoun-Corbet, beloved by all, teaching at last the children of those she had known at her first coming; and her monumental tablet may still be seen under the great east window of the church, now, alas! sadly shorn of its many-colored glories by the hand of time and of violence!

ELIZABETH ELLENWOOD,

Schoolmistress,

AGED SIXTY YEARS.

"Blessed are the dead which die in the Lord yea, saith the Spirit, that they may rest from their labours; and their works do follow them."

www.ingramcontent.com/pod-product-compliance
Lightning Source LLC
Chambersburg PA
CBHW030540130626
46552CB00006B/2354